Echoes of a Fever Dream

J.R. Curtis

For anyone named Craig,
because they probably deserve to win one.

Table of Contents

A Drift

Snow snakes.

Those wispy, winding flurries of snowflakes that cross the road with the wind, slithering over the asphalt in a ghostly dance. Frigid and unwelcoming, but eye-catching and beautiful all the same. A description that could fit almost anything that winter brings. Jagged icicles, blizzards, squalls... all potentially lethal, but awe inspiring in their unrepentant bitterness.

Snap out of it.

"Shit." I gasp, as I fight my steering wheel for control.

The car bucks as I jerk the wheel back to attention and return to the lane. Muted and annoyed vibrations groan up the frame of the vehicle, as the rumble strip meets the tire. Barely a second later, and I'm back in my rightful spot on the road with my heart pounding.

That was too close.

I can hear my pulse in my ears as the adrenaline greets my body in its textbook abruptness.

My eyes are wide open now. The upsetting remembrance of how quickly things can go bad, has shocked my system into paying actual attention.

We can so often be lulled into a false sense of security with our cars. Day after day we arrive at our destination, safe and sound. But what we don't think about, is that our successful navigation is often not a product of our skill, but that of blind luck.

How often have you been driving, only to realize that for some undetermined amount of time, you have been elsewhere? Occupying some distant shelf in the backrooms of our minds, while our hands and feet blindly pilot a two-ton weapon on wheels. I know I have, more often than I would care to admit.

You're doing it again.

I shake my head violently, feeling my brain rattle around. I raise a hand; cold and white knuckled from its relentless grip on the wheel.

Winding up, I strike myself across the cheek. Too soft at first, my instincts refusing to do it hard enough. I wind up again, giving myself a real-good smack across the face.

The sting of it pulls my eyes open, and they water slightly. I blink away the wetness and wipe it off with my sleeve.

It's starting to snow again and it's getting ever darker with each passing minute. I can see my headlights now, reflected back at me off of the endless white, as I travel onward.

I should have stopped at the last town.

It wasn't much of a town, but it had a single level, rundown motel. Even if I refused to sleep on the flea ridden mattress, that was no doubt waiting inside the room, I could have at least slept in my car in the parking lot and weathered the storm.

I glance over at my phone, seeing if *she's* texted me, wondering where I am.

Truthfully, that's why I haven't stopped. I'm too anxious, too nervously excited to get there.

No texts, but no signal either.

If she has texted me, I won't know it til I get out of the boonies. I sigh a little, annoyed at being cut off out here. I eye the empty signal bars a moment longer and return the phone to the seat next to me.

I glance back up at the whirling flakes that are dashing past my accelerating car.

But I'm not actually looking.

My eyes are glazed over, thinking.

"She'll be happy to see you." I think. "Maybe a little reserved at first, but once you apologize... and I mean *really* apologize, you can still salvage a somewhat enjoyable Christmas."

I don't even remember what the fight was about now.

Her father's health had been taking a turn for the worse the latter half of the year, and she'd left a month early to be with him and her family.

Things had been strained between us for most of the year and the added stress of her ailing father had made tempers even shorter.

The day she'd left, we'd fought.

Now, as I drive onward into the night and after her, I'm racked with guilt of what a jackass I was.

Things had come to a head, right as she'd walked out the door. A terrible time to fight.

We'd both walked away angry and what limited interaction we'd had since, had felt like we were somehow strangers now.

Interesting how a nasty enough argument can revert you almost back to the *strangers* stage.

Not strangers in the traditional sense however. You still know everything about each other.

But a mean enough fight can put an invisible wall between you. You can't see it, but you both know it is there. Each fight, each frustrated sigh, each eye roll... They all apply another layer of hard-shell epoxy to your hearts, and finding a way back into them proves even more impossible as time goes on.

God, my gut is turning.

I rub my eyes and roll down the window, desperate for some fresh air. The wind is loud, and instantly deafens me to everything else. Flakes dance into the cab and land upon my face, melting quickly on my flushed cheeks.

I keep it open until I can no longer stand it. Finally relenting a moment later and rolling it back up, shivering.

I turn up the radio. I'm not hopeful at all that any signal will come through. I'm only going through the motions.

Hissing static rises up, just as I thought it would. My fingers hover over the knob to turn it back down again.

What is static? Why does it make that specific noise? Who decided to call it static? Why isn't it just silent if there isn't anything to listen to? Wasn't there some study that if you listen to static long enough, your brain gets bored and starts to make itself hear things in the white noise?

Shit.

The road has curved and I am going entirely too fast to navigate it.

Reflexively, I move the wheel and try to stay on the road. It would have worked too, had it not been for an extra-slippery stretch of piling snow.

The wheel jerks back and forth in my hands and I can feel the rear of the car pitching around in a circle.

Suddenly, I'm not looking ahead. Instead, I'm facing back toward where I've come from.

Not a great feeling.

My car finishes its three quarters donut, stopping at the 270° point and sliding off the road entirely. The car bucks and shakes as my wheels leave the asphalt and send me down a wild, yet brief ride to the bottom of a dirt hill.

A moment later, and I am completely stopped, still gripping the wheel with intense force. A second later, and I come out of the daze. I let go of the wheel and look around, only now taking in exactly where I am.

I'm in a field, parked at the bottom of a steeply sloped hill at the side of the road.

The car is still running, and honestly, in tip top shape. An alignment will no doubt be needed at some point after my wild ride down the hill, but other than that, the car is fine.

I look ahead, out into the field. I squint past the wiper blades that are frantically battling the ever intensifying snowstorm.

Ahead, across several hundred feet of flat pasture, thick woods dot the horizon. I sigh, hoping to have seen a house or a barn that would indicate other people.

I haven't even pressed the gas, and I know for a fact that I'm not getting out of this field without a tow.

I button up the jacket I'm wearing, fastening the top button tightly against my neck. I take a deep breath and push open the driver's door.

With the first step out into the beyond, I sink in the snow up to my knees. Cold powder fills my shoes and I immediately want to return to the warm capsule of the car.

I shut the door behind me and begin to climb the hill back to the road.

It goes about as well as is expected. For every four steps that give me some sort of progression, the fifth step sends me sliding back to the mark of the first step.

By some miracle, I finally crest the hill.

Sweating and shivering at the same time, I gasp for air as the cold burns my lungs and throat.

A moment later, when I've composed myself as much as I am able, I cast my glance this way and that down the opposite ends of the road. Melting snow drips down from my hair and runs off the end of my nose.

Jesus, it's really coming down now.

Getting colder with every passing second, I relent from my perch at the top and begin to descend back to the refuge of my car.

It's still running.

Exhaust bellows visibly from the tailpipe as I make clumsy, wide steps toward the driver's door.

The wipers are still rolling back and forth noisily, as I flop into my seat and slam the door shut. I shiver, rubbing my hands together. I shake my head and let the snow and water tumble down.

I pick up my phone and glance first at the time, and then to the signal bars.

FUCK!

I slam my palm into the cold steering wheel again and again, screaming as I do so.

This was my one chance. This was supposed to go perfectly. I'm supposed to be there, the shoulder to cry on. I want to be there. I want to be there for her.

Minutes later, with my chest heaving and the anger relenting into a muted aggression, I exhale and succumb to the situation.

What other choice do I have?

I sit back, reaching below and gripping the cold plastic to recline the seat. As I slink backward, I watch the landing flakes, hating them.

I watch them for a long time. Fat, engorged, snowflakes anchoring onto the windshield and melting mere seconds later.

Like counting sheep, the activity has a sort of numbing effect on my mind. I can feel my eyes fluttering shut and I welcome it.

Sleep is the closest thing the human race has to time travel, and in this instance, I welcome it with open arms.

I'll wake up in a few hours when the storm stops.

Something catches my eye.

Far, across the field, at the front row of the dense forest beyond, there is something that wasn't there before.

Probably nothing.

I squint and try to focus my vision to understand exactly what I'm seeing.

It looks like... a person.

A shape, far beyond my marooned car, at the base of the trees... stands a figure.

Definitely not.

I squint even harder, as if that will yield a different result.

It's too far to tell for certain. It's black and shadowy in the blur of distance, but the shape of the outline does suggest a person.

I shake my head and huff out a breath. Leaning back, I close my eyes and hope for sleep, stubbornly.

It wasn't a person. Remember when you went camping in scouts? There was a figure standing out in the clearing just like you're seeing now. What did that turn out to be? A horse, turning its head and eating grass. A trick of the light and a fib from the angle.

Lay down and sleep.

Leave it alone.

My eyes shoot open. I sit back up and squint again.

This is the dumbest thing you've ever been worried about.

It's still there, but it's... closer?

Impossible.

But it is. Whatever I was seeing, was indeed somehow, closer.

A shadow.

Still too far away to visually dissect, but closer nonetheless. I straighten myself and keep my eyes locked onto the whatever-it-is at the edge of the trees.

I stare at it, for what must be five minutes straight.

Still it does not move.

"Hmph." I breathe to myself, satisfied.

Though my own noise startles me more than I care to admit.

I lay back down, staring at the dirty gray of the car's ceiling. I let my eyes drift closed and after many more minutes of restless twisting in my brain, sleep finally comes.

II

My eyes drift open and for a moment, I am very afraid. Though, I do not know why.

Perhaps, it is because of the unfamiliar sight of the car's roof, and for a moment, I forget where I am.

Or, maybe it is the inkling of a fading nightmare I do not fully recall.

Either way, my chest is tight and my breathing is rapid.

I sit up and look around.

It is dark, too dark.

It cannot already be night, can it?

I blink and glance around. Reaching up, I flip the switch for the cab light and I am instantly bathed in glowing yellowish-white.

With this, I can now see what the problem is.

The windows are completely buried in snow, allowing no light in whatsoever.

I reach and switch on the wipers, thinking that I hadn't turned them off in the first place.

The plastic blades struggle for a moment under the weight of the snow. But finally, they pull through, launching white back and forth in an angry torrent.

It's darker outside, but not *full night*. Evening is still in the middle of its shift, a little ways from clocking out and giving night the keys.

With that situation sorted, my bladder speaks up, informing me of another pressing issue. I pull the latch to my door and push.

The door barely budges. Snow is piled high, all the way up to the window outside. Putting more weight into it, I finally manage to squeak the door open just enough to shimmy out and stand on the edge of the car's door frame.

Jesus.

A slightly maddening memory floats into frame.

I recall a moment from when I was a kid. A time when CDs were still used, rather than decorating dusty shelves in old closets, waiting to either be donated or thrown away.

There was a CD I'd had then, one that I'd burned a mishmash of songs onto.

One of the tracks was a very popular one-hit-wonder, though I cannot remember the name now.

One day, I'd tried to play the CD and it had somehow gotten scratched. About a quarter of the way into this particular song, the CD refused to continue further, and instead chose to repeat a particular line over and over again. Playing it rapidly and almost like a nightmare.

"...And they don't stop comin'/ And they don't stop comin'/And they don't stop comin'/And they don't stop comin'/And they don't stop comin'..."

I laugh a little to myself. "Why..." I wonder, "...did I think of that?"

But as I look up and observe the still unrelenting snow, I suppose it fits.

I finish urinating and zip my pants back up just in time for my eyes to catch something across the field.

Terror strikes me with a delayed fuse.

My eyes notice and process what they are seeing, but my brain is a few milliseconds late in telling me. Like a five second delay in broadcast television.

The shadow, the dark-thing, is closer now, much closer than before.

Now, bathed in the muted glow of my buried headlights, there can be no question.

I no longer have the luxury of writing it off as a trick of the light. It *is* a figure, standing in the clearing.

It faces me, but is faceless. A dark hood is pulled up over itself, hiding any sort of visible features.

Unsure of what else to do, I simply shrink backward into the car, moving in slow motion as I do so.

I slip into the driver's seat and creak the door shut beside me.

Car doors cannot be shut quietly, if one closes it softly, it only half latches. A synchronized ding begins to sound, letting me know the door is ajar. I pay it no mind.

My eyes are forward, alert, scanning the clearing for the thing I just saw.

But I cannot see it.

Though my eyes grope the darkness outside, they can find nothing.

I remember it then, the cab light is still on.

Light in darkness comes with a price.

Whether in our homes, cars, or camps; if we are bathed in light, the void can see us much better. We are blind to the unknown terrors outside, as we stand in our oasis of light, and we are picked apart by whatever things may watch us from the dark.

A lit window in the night is a porthole for whatever gazes, to gaze as it likes.

I reach up and flip the light off. My eyes adjust, and a moment later I can see outside again.

It's closer.

Somehow, it is so much closer in just the few seconds I had not watched it.

I stare, watching that humanoid absence of light, until my eyes burn and beg me to blink.

It does not sway, or move. It does not breathe, or shiver visibly. It only stands, post-like and observing my stranded car.

Dryness like fire burns my eyes and tears well up, falling down my cheeks.

I relent, blinking as quickly as I can manage. My stinging eyes darken and refocus, as the lids slide over the dried orbs like sand.

Closer still.

It is merely ten feet from my car now. Standing, and unrelenting in its watch.

A deep, primal panic begins to brew in my stomach. Bubbling acid of fear, rising to meet my thundering heart.

I am going to leave the car. I don't know how, and I don't know where I will go. But there is not a choice in this matter. Come what may, I am going to rip open the door and scramble up the hill as fast as I can.

Another blink. Involuntary and unplanned.

I wipe my eyes frantically and cast my gaze forward again, searching for the thing. But it is not there anymore.

Tap. Tap. Tap.

A sickening turn of my gut follows the sudden and ghostly sound. My head rips to the side, locking sight on the shadow that raps at my passenger window.

A silent scream looses from my throat. A hollow, hiss of air unaided by paralyzed vocal cords.

Somehow, my hand finds the latch to my door. I tear it open, battering the snow back and stumbling out into the night.

I don't look back. I don't allow myself even a millisecond of pause. I am scrambling, clawing, and leaping up the hill as fast as I can. My throat burns from the exertion and my legs sting at the steep incline.

At any moment, I expect to feel cold fingers grasp the back of my neck and drag me down.

It is a universal feeling of involuntary panic, felt since the first human scrambled away from darkness.

Out of a cave, up the stairs, sprinting away from neutral black. Terrified and not knowing exactly why.

By some sort of divine intervention, I reach the road.

By another miracle, I am suddenly bathed in the headlights of an approaching vehicle. I look up, shielding my eyes from the beams.

I hear a horn sound and brakes squeal.

A moment later, and a semi truck sits before me with its engine chugging lowly.

"Jesus! You okay?" A voice asks from the dark cab.

I don't respond. I jump to my feet and run to the passenger side. I tear open the door and climb the steps inside.

The cab light is on now, and I can see the driver.

A middle aged man, bald and with a large bushy beard, stares back at me.

I watch his expression go from confused, to fearful. Almost as if, the face I am surely wearing myself, was contagious and immediately spread to his own.

"Go!" Is all I can manage to hoarsely shout. I shut the door and collapse into the seat, shivering and wheezing.

He doesn't have to be told twice. Gulping hard, his eyes return to the road and he puts the truck into gear.

Still gasping, I look out the window toward the field as we begin to roll.

The shadow is gone. All that's left is my car, alone in the field with the beam of its headlights cast adrift in the night.

"You okay?" A voice hovers by my ears.

I don't hear it at first, only pieces. Like a mosquito buzzing by; only audible in intervals. I'm still staring off, watching trees roll past the window.

"Hey. Are you alright?" I hear clearly, finally.

"Yeah." I manage, in a choked whisper.

"You mind telling me what's going on? What you were running from?" The guy asks, shooting me intermittent glances as he watches the road.

"I slid off the road a few hours ago. Lost control." I reply.

"No. Not that. Why were you sprinting into the road, wide eyed like a maniac? You're not on drugs or something..." He asks, trailing off.

I look over to meet his eyes. He's staring me down, sizing me up.

"No. No drugs." I assure him. "I was waiting out the storm and someone came out of the woods. They were staring me down... and they started attacking me, trying to get into the car." I finish, adding the last part as an afterthought; a little sane pinch of sugar to help the crazy truth go down.

"Jesus." He says after a bit. "Really? You sure it wasn't an animal? Somebody would have to be ratshit crazy to be all the way out here."

"Not an animal." I say.

He whistles out a sigh and shakes his head.

"I'm Virgil, by the way." He says after a minute.

"Hey, Virgil." I reply and give him my name in return.

"Maniac hiding out in the woods. That's a new one, even for here." Virgil says.

I ask him what he means by "here".

"Bad place, this." He continues. "I try to avoid coming through these parts whenever I can, but it always seems to happen one way or another. There always seems to be something strange happening on this stretch of road. Some things I've seen, some things they've told me about." He finishes, tapping on his CB radio.

"Like what?" I ask, politely curious, but also believing him much more than I want to.

"I was coming through once, and I came around this corner... Next thing I knew, I was face to face with a roaring inferno. Not a wildfire, though. A bus, a school bus. It was ablaze with flames that were taller than the trees. I slammed on the brakes and skittered to a halt just past it. But when I stepped out, the whole damn thing was gone... I coulda' chalked it up to just one of those things. You know? ...But you know how when you look at something real bright, and when you blink you can still sorta see it?... Well, that made it kinda hard to dismiss."

He clears his throat and hocks tobacco juice into a cup.

"Another time..." He starts up again. "My buddy Charon." He taps the CB. "He told me about this time he came through here. Said he was driving and he could see these funny shapes hanging in the air in the distance. Said he thought it might've been birds at first. But when he got closer... He swears it was people. About fifty people floating in the air, hanging from rope around their necks. Rope that just went up into the sky as far as he could see. But with a blink, they were gone, just like the bus."

I breathe loudly, noticing that my heart is pounding.

My thoughts suddenly turn to her.

"How far is Sunrise?" I ask, eager to change the subject.

"Sunrise? Oh at the rate we're going... I'd say, maybe another seven or eight miles, we're real close. Is that where you're heading? You spun off the road in the home stretch."

"Really?!" I ask, shocked.

"Sure enough." He says.

Is it possible I was that close?

I suppose it is.

I was spacing in and out for so long, I must've gotten mixed up.

Fear melts away slightly and excitement begins to replace it.

I'm going to make it, despite the shit show that the last several hours have been, I'm going to make it.

He spits in his cup again, sniffing before he breaks the silence.

"What's in Sunrise?" He asks.

"A girl." I say. "No, *the* girl." I correct myself quickly.

"Ah." He says, nodding. "That'd explain why you were trying to drive through this storm. Christmas or no Christmas, a storm like this... and a car like yours... You shoulda stayed put."

"If it wasn't important, I would have." I say back, meandering over images of her in my thoughts.

"Hey buddy, for a girl? Nuff said." He chortles a little and spits into the cup again. "Myself? Once I finish this route, I'll be heading home for the holidays too. Once the storm clears of course."

I nod, but don't reply as he continues.

The trees sail by outside. They are dark, even despite the white powder that covers them thickly.

I wonder absently to myself.

We pass these thick woods all the time. Cruising past the walls of towering pine, without a second thought.

But how far back do the columns go?

For all that we know, they could stretch out for infinity. Endless towering shelves of wood, leading out into the darkness and the unknown beyond.

Who has seen the edge of the world?

My thoughts slow and stop, just as the trees passing outside do. I look up, confused at the reason for our slowing.

I first glance at Virgil. His eyes are cast forward, looking at the road. My eyes move to see what he is fixed on. As I see what he sees, I feel my stomach become concrete.

Standing out in the center of the darkened road, is the shadow thing.

I try to shout to Virgil, but my tongue has turned suddenly to lead.

He stops.

I can't believe my eyes. But he is opening the door, stepping out, and walking to meet the thing.

"Hey pal! You scared the hell out of me!" I hear him calling ahead to it. "What're you standing out in the middle of the road for?"

I watch as he walks out in front of the truck, trudging through the snow and shielding his face from the howling flakes with an outstretched arm.

Frozen, sealed in utter terror, I sit.

I cannot move. I cannot call out to him to warn him.

"Come on over to the truck, you'll freeze to dea-"

Virgil's voice cuts out. But not because the thing attacked, and not because he saw something that stole his words.

Virgil's voice cuts out because *Virgil cuts out.*

It is the only way I can explain what I see. In the passing of milliseconds, Virgil has completely vanished from existence.

One moment, he is standing there, calling out to the thing in black.

Another, and he is gone.

Blank air replaces him, asserting that the man called Virgil was never there at all.

The shock of such an upsetting sight pulls me out of my stupor. Frozen a moment before, insanity has cracked a steel chair over my head and shaken me loose.

I move almost involuntarily. I jump across the truck and into the driver's seat, just as the thing outside begins to raise its cloaked face.

I slam Virgil's door, looking at the massive gear shift to my right.

I've driven stick before, how hard could it be?

I push the shift into *hopefully* the right gear. I ease off the clutch and the truck lurches forward, grinding and bellowing at the misoperation. I tap the gas with my foot gingerly, not daring to push it harder, lest it kill the engine.

I look up and the thing is closer, standing just in front of the grill of the truck. The void of its face stares through the windscreen and into me.

I scream, gripping the wheel tightly and crawling forward at a snail's pace. The thing refuses to take its gaze from me, and I from it.

The truck continues forward and the thing dissipates like air into the hood.

I tremble in shock and horror, looking at my feet. I am sure that at any second it will phase through the floor and pull me down with it.

But it doesn't.

Because as far as I can tell, the thing is gone.

Thank God.

The truck keeps creeping on, lurching and grinding as it does.

But it doesn't stall and it doesn't stop. It continues on, puttering down the blackened highway under the towering trees. Snow dances past the headlights and I hold tightly to the wheel, steering the truck onward at barely five miles an hour.

I keep going.

On and on I drive through the howling fury outside, squinting at the dotted line and doing my best to hold the rig centered.

As more time passes, I become convinced that pieces of the snow covering the trees are actually milky white eyes, gazing out from beneath dusted branches.

The cab light is not on in here. Nonetheless I feel naked and exposed to whatever may eye me from the dark. Each passing minute is excruciating and my back begs me to stop hunching over the wheel.

An hour passes, maybe two.

I snap from my glazed stare, and see an exit.

Miraculously, it is the exact exit I need.

I turn the wheel and the frame of the rig growls as I cross the rumble strips.

I take a side street.

I turn once, then again.

It's there.

Somehow, someway, the house is there, right before my eyes. *Her* house.

The numbers of the address are carved into a decorative boulder adorned with Christmas lights. The address is correct, I know it for certain.

Just then, with impeccable timing, the truck grinds to a labored halt and dies. Dull grinding and sputtering sounds from underneath the hood and I decide that it will likely never be driven again.

The cab door squeaks as I push it open and half-step, half-fall out of the driver's seat.

I stand up, taking in the full display of the house.

Christmas ornaments and lights decorate the yard and the dwelling beyond. Red, green, and white lights, twinkling beautifully against the handfuls of loose flakes that windmill from the sky.

Orange and yellow glows from behind drawn shades of the house; warm and welcoming.

It is the single most beautiful sight I have ever seen.

Despite myself, I feel like crying.

Warm tears leak from my eyes and chill seconds later, freezing my cheeks and rolling off of my chin.

I take a step, and then another. Snow crunches underfoot as I approach the oasis among the frost.

As I reach the porch and begin to ascend the icy stairs, an all-encompassing, incredible feeling of peace envelops me.

Sanctuary awaits me on the other side of the door and I feel anticipation of this surety embrace me in a tight and tender hug.

A feeling I have never experienced before; I am not afraid.

I grip the handle of the door.

It's time to head in.

III

Somewhere, along a nondescript stretch of highway in rural America, a police cruiser drove.

It was the morning after a particularly nasty winter storm and the cruiser was still covered in heavy snow, aside from the windows.

"No, no. That was the *series finale* last night. Not the season, the show's done. Kaput." Officer Welsh said to his partner; Officer Fields.

"Really?" Fields asked, incredulously. "That was the ending? Could've fooled me. It sure as hell didn't feel like an ending."

Welsh shrugged. "That's what I read. I didn't make the show."

Fields grumbled, taking a cautious sip of his coffee that was still far too hot. His tongue felt raw from an overconfident sip he'd had a few minutes before.

"Why do they do that?" He asked after a few more seconds. "Get you all involved and invested in something good-"

"Hang on." Welsh interjected. His eyes were squinting out through the frosted windshield at the road.

Fields looked, trying to see what Welsh was seeing, but saw nothing.

"There." Welsh said with an outstretched finger. Slowing the car down, he put it in park and hopped out onto the side of the highway.

"You mind telling me what the hell you're looking at?" Fields called ahead to Welsh who was already far ahead.

Eventually, Fields caught up to him.

Welsh was standing at the edge of the road, looking down at a large lump, buried in snow.

"It's a car." Fields muttered to Welsh, finally understanding.

"Yeah. Let's see if anybody's home." Welsh replied, stepping over a large snowbank and starting the half-walk, half-slide down the hill.

Begrudgingly, Fields began the descent also. On the first step, his boot filled almost entirely with snow and he wished that he had listened to his wife and worn his snow pants.

Welsh was at the side of the car shaped lump now. Brushing snow from it, he called out to whoever may be inside. "Hello!? Anyone in here? You alright?" He spoke out blindly, still unable to see through the frosted windows.

With some effort, Welsh found the handle to the car door and pulled.

Much to his and Fields' horror, as the door was drawn back, a frozen corpse fell out along with it.

A young man, pale and frost covered, lay dead.

His limp form rested against Welsh, who somehow managed to not scream. He simply sighed and pushed the corpse back to rest on the driver's seat headrest.

"Jesus." Fields huffed. "What the hell happened to him?"

Welsh thought on this for a moment, but the answer came quickly.

"The car's still running." He informed Fields, matter-of-factly. "The snow held all the exhaust in. He suffocated."

"Poor bastard." Fields muttered, feeling the sparse contents of his stomach turning.

"No." Welsh replied. "I'd say he's one of the lucky ones. In fact, when my time comes Fields, that's how I wanna go. Peacefully, in my sleep."

The Emptiness of Time

SUBMITTED FOR CONSIDERATION FOR THE DIGITIZING OF THE LIBRARY'S CATALOG

ITEM:23776
TITLE:UNKNOWN
DESCRIPTION:A LOOSE ASSORTMENT OF HANDWRITTEN NOTES BOUND TOGETHER
LOCATION:TUCKED BETWEEN TWO ENCYCLOPEDIAS IN THE NONFICTION SECTION 500-531
ORIGIN: UNKNOWN

TRANSCRIPTION:

I am unsure how to begin this letter, or how long it will be when I am done.

I suppose I have all the time in the world, so I can write it however I see fit.

I'm also unsure if this writing will ever be read by anyone, this entire exercise may be entirely futile… But, "fuck it" I suppose, would be the proper expression in this instance.

When we have considered or fantasized about time travel throughout human history, we often picture meeting those we would otherwise have no natural means of ever being introduced to.

Or perhaps we hope to see nearly fantastical or significant historical events.

I am here to tell you that reality does not yield this result.

In fact, based on my findings, the end result of the often chased "time travel", is in reality quite grim, and I suppose rather dull.

Now, at this point if anyone has somehow picked up this assortment of scratch paper and continued to read thus far, you are no doubt rolling your eyes after the last paragraph.

It makes no difference to me whether you believe it or not though. I am stuck here, and I wish now that I had never come.

I was a scientist, in the now far off year of 2274. After many failures, I finally cracked the elusive code behind the long speculated science.

I won't tell you how, because no one should ever try it.

This writing is my attempt to dissuade any future readers of these notes from trying it, however small the possibility and effectiveness their attempt might have.

Traveling backward in time does not take you to watch the pyramids being built, or to see medieval battles clash before you in real time.

The pyramids are here and so too are the fields that once held such bloody, medieval carnage.

But anyone and anything living, is not here at all.

Streets are bare, houses empty. Cars litter the streets, parked in the spots they were once left in.

But not a bird or even a fly exists in this hollow realm.

I started off small. Traveling to the 1950s.

I've always been partial to the aesthetic of that era, both in fashion and in automobiles. I am here now, and have seen plenty of both, but I am the only living soul that exists in this plane.

My theory, simplified, is this; Imagine time is a train. Currently, you are riding on said train.

Fifty or one hundred feet back on the tracks, is the place you were five or ten years ago. These metaphorical tracks stretch on and on through time and eternity itself.

You could jump off of this train and stroll backward to where you were existing at one point in time, but all that is living is coasting beyond you, hurtling forward through their limited ride.

I exist in this hollow place now, a traveler without a destination.

Food is plentiful and there are many creature comforts to enjoy in solitude.

But I cannot get out of this place and no inkling of life is here to keep company with.

So I warn you now, dear reader, do not look back.

STATUS: REJECTED

OTHER NOTES: WHO WROTE THIS? THIS WAS GREAT FOR A LAUGH.

The Grass is Greener

Along a darkened corridor he walked, passing broken picture frames and peeling walls.

A dim yellow light was coming from somewhere behind him, at the end of the filthy hall. Long, arching shadows were cast sharply along the ruined carpet and walls. A pit of dread was rooted deeply in his stomach and pulsed out in waves, chilling his arms and pounding in his head. His breathing felt shallow and labored. He had to keep going.

He was trying to get away from something, but he didn't know what. Not daring to run, for fear that the sound would give him away. He padded cautiously and carefully along.

The hall seemed to stretch on forever and he could not remember where he had come from, nor where he was actually going. He only knew that he couldn't stop and he didn't dare look back.

A shadow that was not his own crossed over the yellowish light and he knew that it had found him. A horrible chill washed over him and he kept his head facing forward, refusing to look at how close it was behind him.

He cut sideways, into the nearest room. Carefully, he closed the door softly and winced at each creak and crack as it shut.

It was a bathroom, or it once was before it had fallen into its current, disgusting state of decay. The mirror was shattered, though large reflective shards still clung to the wall. The floor was covered in trash, dirty needles, and other wet, unrecognizable masses. The toilet, long overflowed, sat caked and crusted over every inch, giving off a nauseating aroma of methane. The smell permeated his nostrils and wet his mouth with a teasing vomit.

Footsteps passed outside and he held his breath even more.

He watched the crack at the bottom of the door intensely, waiting for the shadow outside to return and stop.

He waited for the rusted doorknob to rattle, and for the door to burst open.

But it didn't, and he was left alone again.

As he stepped forward to leave and to try and double back behind the thing, a shard of shimmering glass caught his eye.

Suddenly, he was struck with the unrelenting desire to look into the mirror. He didn't know why, but he followed the feeling and turned to face the glass.

It was too dark.

He stared into the largest shard of the broken mirror and couldn't make out anything of his face, other than the silhouette.

He stepped back, slowly grabbing the doorknob.

Shrinking back as it creaked, he crept the door open just a bit. Yellow light poured into the room and he could see much better.

This time, he moved much slower toward the mirror. He stared into the shard of glass and inspected his face.

It was normal enough. His hair was full and long, though very greasy and in desperate need of a wash. His eyes were a light blue, peering out from tired sockets and almost glittering against the dull light. His nose bore a scar across the bridge that disappeared into his slightly gaunt cheeks. His lips were scarred here and there, as they always had been; thanks to his incessant chewing of them when anxiety came creeping.

He didn't look ugly. If anything, he just looked dirty, and hungry.

So why had he felt the need to stare at his reflection in the mirror?

Another instinct, more regretful than the first, pushed him to open his mouth and look within.

His eyes flicked down toward the slit of his closed mouth and he watched as he lowered his jaw.

He immediately wished that he hadn't.

A crimson mixture of saliva and blood dripped out, falling into the sink and leaving strands on the dirty stubble that decorated his chin.

His heart jumped in his chest and terror pumped against the inside of his skull with what he saw next.

Teeth.

His teeth fell out of his gaping mouth, lolling down with more strands of stringy blood. But they didn't fall into the sink, they stopped, just below his chin.

It was then that he saw what had been done to his mouth.

Every single tooth was removed, roots and all. The teeth dangled from his gums, crudely stitched into them with thin medical thread. Each tooth was drilled through and knotted to a separate strand of thread that swung from his puffed gums like Christmas tree ornaments. Some were tangled, pulling on the stitchings of others. He restrained his jaw as much as he could, trying not to yank the gore free.

A horrified moan came from somewhere deep, down in his bowels. More spit and blood drooled down as he stared.

A shadow crossed his shoulders behind him and in the shard of mirror, he was brought face to face with it.

Gasping and thrashing against the sheets that held him down, David screamed.

Soft white light met his eyes and stayed his frantic cries. He looked around, unsure of where he was.

He looked down. Soft and clean white sheets lay over his legs and stomach.

He looked up. Cream colored columns of a poster bed climbed upward, dangling translucent fabric from their corners. Birds chirped faintly outside and the sun shone softly through the curtains over the window.

A woman appeared at the door then, and David's eyes met hers, still a little afraid. But he knew almost instantly where he was and who she was.

It was Abbey, his wife.

She was holding a tray of food and looking concerned at David.

"Hon?" She asked, quizzically. "Are you alright?"

"Yeah." David said, sharply exhaling and rubbing his eyes. "Just a bad dream." He offered a smile to seal the reassurance.

Her eyes did not return the expression and she furrowed a brow. She set down the tray of food and walked to press her hand to his forehead.

"You're sweating." Abbey sighed. "Dammit. I told Dr. Costley you weren't ready to come home. I'll go get him on the phone, right now."

"No, really. I'm fine." David said, taking her arm. "It was just a nightmare. I promise."

Abbey stepped back and looked into his eyes for a moment, judging what she saw.

"If you're sure..." She said after a moment, cautiously. Her brow relaxed and she sighed. "You know, you don't have to be so tough all the time right? Just don't overdo it. I need you." She gave him a sideways smile and tilted her head as she looked into his eyes.

"I know." He replied with a smile.

He took her shoulder and pulled her down into the bed, holding her tightly. She draped an arm over him and nuzzled her head above his shoulder.

"I'm alright." David soothed. "Everything's good upstairs, baby."

She lowered her head onto his chest and felt his heartbeat, still slowing from the nightmare, but steady.

"Ok." David interjected, breaking the silence that had held. "Whatever you have over there smells amazing." He said, gesturing with his head to where she had left the tray.

Abbey smiled, letting out a quiet laugh.

"I'm sure it tastes even better." David said, grunting as he swiveled to get to his feet.

Abbey caught his shoulder and pulled him back down, climbing on top of him.

"How does this taste?" She asked, letting her hair tickle his bare chest as she lowered her lips to meet his.

They kissed passionately, as David wrapped his arms around her. Abbey raised her head, locking eyes with him and seemingly awaiting an answer.

"I mean, I did see bacon on that tray." David replied playfully with a shrug.

"Oh, shut up!" Abbey gasped out, punching him, and beginning to laugh.

Breakfast had been eaten and Abbey had gone back downstairs.

Now, David stood underneath the showerhead. He could feel muscles relaxing as the warm stream washed over him. His stomach was full and he felt incredibly well rested. For some reason, he felt that he had never been more content in his entire life.

He stayed in the shower for a long time, only leaving when the water began to dip in temperature.

Stepping out of the shower, he fetched a towel and began to dry with it. He thought that he had never felt something so soft.

Standing now before the mirror; a large and pristine sheet of glass, he wiped the steam from it.

The face that stared back at him from the reflection, was a far cry from the twisted and gaunt ghost he had been acquainted with in his nightmare.

He looked good, handsome even. He allowed himself a little more vanity and examined his features in the soft light, enjoying the familiar and friendly face that looked back.

Downstairs, the doorbell rang.

Thinking that Abbey would get it, he looked away from the mirror and retrieved his toothbrush.

The doorbell rang again, sounding much more insistent this time. Whoever was outside was pushing the button, but allowing their touch to linger on the bell.

It was an annoying sound.

"Honey?!" David called out, his mouth full of toothpaste and garbling his voice.

No answer came from downstairs, aside from another incessant press of the doorbell.

David spit, followed by an annoyed sigh. He wiped his lips and went out into the hallway. Still clutching the towel that was wrapped around his waist, he descended the stairs.

Again the doorbell rang, just as David was grasping the knob and pulling the door open.

The man outside still had his hand outstretched, withdrawing back from the button. His face looked embarrassed, as if he'd been caught reaching into the cookie jar.

"Yeah?" David asked, trying not to sound *too* upset, but not entirely pleasant either.

"Good day sir." The man outside said.

He looked out at David from beneath a finely maintained black panama hat, and he wore a neatly pressed suit with white around the collar.

A preacher.

David stared back at him, confused.

"Uh, hi." He offered.

"Have you heard the truth?" The Preacher inquired.

David felt his eyes drift up into a roll at the question.

He sighed. "Look, pal. You've kind of caught me at a bad time. I'm still in my towel."

Undeterred, the Preacher kept up his spiel. "God cares not about the appearance of his sheep. Only that those of his flock return home!"

"Hey, that's great." David muttered. "I think I'll take a rain check on all of that though, Father."

The Preacher didn't slow down, he instead spoke louder, as if persistence and volume would somehow net a different result.

"The truth is here!" He nearly shouted. "You must only reach out and take it! These trappings and comforts of our lives are falsehoods! Do not fall prey to the lies!"

What little patience David had held onto until this moment, evaporated. He slammed the door in the man's face with little regret.

"Nut job." He mumbled to himself.

He returned to the bedroom upstairs and finally dressed himself. He shaved, combed his hair, and made his way downstairs.

He reached the kitchen, and sat down at the table.

Just then, Abbey entered from the backyard.

She was wearing a sun hat and gardening gloves, removing them both as she came in. Turning around, she closed the sliding glass door.

"Was someone at the door a while ago?" She asked, tossing the question over her shoulder at David, who still sat in the kitchen.

"Yeah. Some Jesus-freak. I practically had to push him out of the door to slam it."

Abbey shook her head. "Oh, God. I saw him roaming around the far end of the neighborhood earlier."

She raised her hands and shook them a little comedically. "*End of days...*"

"I guess so." David said, with a shrug and a laugh.

Abbey made her way into the kitchen. She washed her hands at the sink and opened several pill bottles. She selected one pill from each bottle and placed them all into a small paper cup. She rounded the counter and approached David, offering him the cup.

"What's this?" David asked, taking it and examining the contents.

"Antibiotics." Abbey replied. "I know the fever is gone. But the Doc said you've got to take them 'til they're gone."

"Ah. Ok." David nodded, stroking his chin. "Thank you Dr. Abbey." He bowed, dramatically and lowered the cup as an offering.

"You're a real dork. You know that?" Abbey said, shaking her head and suppressing a grin. She left the kitchen and made her way up the stairs to clean herself up.

David watched her go, grinning like an idiot and still holding the cup full of pills.

When she had gone, he tilted the small cup upward to toss them into his mouth. But when the paper met his lips, he miscalculated and ended up tossing them too low to catch them.

The pills went skittering downward, bouncing off of his shirt and rolling onto the floor.

As tends to happen, the dropped objects went immediately into the worst possible spot.

The rolling pills met the open grate of an air conditioning vent, and rolled inside, bouncing away into the guts of the house.

"Shit." David huffed, dropping to his knees and removing the grate.

He peered inside the dark and dusty opening, reaching past the screws that held it in place. He could not see any pills to reach for, and a moment later, he shook his head and returned the vent cover.

He looked up, Abbey was nowhere in sight. Upstairs, he could faintly hear the shower running.

He shrugged, standing up from the vent. He strode across the room and deposited himself into the couch and flipped on the T.V.

He grabbed the remote, and sat back, beginning to mindlessly change channels.

He stopped on one, and allowed himself to zone-out. The events of the day had worn him out more than he'd realized.

Before long, he was just staring at the screen, not paying much attention to the scene that was playing out in front of him.

Time passed, but how much he did not know.

Gradually, the picture in front of him began to slip.

Bit by bit, the scene began to change.

One moment, the T.V. in front of him was playing out a confrontation, where a cartoon bear was angrily chasing a cartoon woodpecker.

Steam hissed from the bear's ears as he stomped along, grabbing the woodpecker around the neck.

The woodpecker gulped as the bear smacked him on top of the head, and a comically sized goose-egg began to rise from under the feathers atop his skull.

In the next moment, the picture flashed.

The T.V. was not there anymore. But a close fight still continued in the spot where it had been.

The woodpecker and the bear were gone.

In their place; two men, covered in bruises and cuts, fought brutally.

One held the other by the throat with one hand, and mercilessly struck him with the other that was balled up into a tight fist.

Again and again he struck the man.

David, who was just beginning to process what he was seeing, recoiled back in horror.

The strikes were vicious, wet, cracking sounds. Not unlike a tenderizer hammering a tough steak.

Blows continued to bash the man's nose, until the bridge and nostrils were combined, mashed into an unrecognizable pulp of blood and gore.

The victim's knees turned to jelly under the weight of his body and he collapsed to the floor in a heap.

The other man climbed on top of him then, straddling the unconscious body.

"Don't..." David heard himself whisper out. Though it came out more like a squeak.

Whether the man had heard him or cared, he couldn't tell, as he didn't stop or turn around.

Instead, he reached his fingers toward the man's eye sockets, and plunged his fingers inside with an audible squelch.

David made a noise, somewhere between a gasp and a gag, and the man raiding the corpse continued his work.

His fingers wiggled inside the puffed openings, as blood and white viscous ooze seeped out around them.

A moment later, the man turned to face David. He lifted his hands, raising the brutalized eyeballs in front of his own, in a mocking, grinning gesture. He smiled, and then popped the crushed, jellied eyes into his mouth, and visually relished the treat.

David screamed.

He wailed and shouted hysterically, shrinking back into the couch and grabbing a nearby pillow to cover his eyes.

A second later, a hand was gripping his shoulder and shaking him. He screamed more, certain that he was next to be brutalized by the eye-eater.

"David!" Abbey screamed.

Her voice, familiar, was enough to pull him from his hysteria. He lowered the pillow cautiously, and looked around the room.

He was back, if he had ever left.

He sat on the sofa, with the T.V. in front of him.

On the screen now, the cartoon bear stood above the cartoon woodpecker, beating his chest. Tiny stars flew around the dazed bird on the ground and his tongue lolled out the side of his beak.

Abbey was holding him now. She placed a hand on his cheek that she used to tilt his gaze toward hers. "David? What's wrong? You were screaming."

It took him a minute.

He gulped in air, trying to calm his fluttering heart.

"I'm fine." He said. "It's nothing."

"It didn't sound like nothing. I don't think I've ever heard you scream like that." Abbey pressed.

"No, really." David replied, getting more of his composure back. "I must've fallen asleep. I guess I still had another nightmare in the bank."

Abbey's eyes watched his for a moment longer, seemingly looking behind them. Her brow tilted, ascertaining if her "dearly-beloved-husband" was in fact, actually alright.

She sighed. "It will get better hon, I promise."

David swallowed, and took another look at the T.V.

"I sure hope it will." He thought.

"Dinner's ready." Abbey informed him.

"I'm not hungry." David replied, wiping his forehead.

"David." Abbey said sternly. "You're white as a sheet and dripping in sweat. I'm not asking. Come and eat."

He allowed himself to smile a little, and stood up. "Well, if it's the doctor's orders..."

As he crossed the threshold into the kitchen, the smell met him immediately and it was incredible. A smorgasbord of aromas, juicy meat, buttery mashed potatoes, steamed vegetables; salted and peppered to perfection.

His mouth watered and his stomach growled, almost saying, "We've been starving, but we didn't want to make a fuss about it until now."

He sat down immediately, pulling a chair back with a squeak and almost jumping into it.

Abbey, already sitting down and waiting for David, smiled as she watched him dig in.

"I thought you weren't hungry." She teased.

David swallowed.

The food tasted even better than it had smelled and he couldn't eat it fast enough.

"Yeah. When you're right you're right." He replied before scooping up another spoonful.

Abbey sat back, resigning to sip at some wine rather than eat. "I went to Marcia's today. She and Lucas are going to Cancun in two months. She asked if I could water their plants."

"Uh-huh." David nodded without looking up.

"I said sure..." Abbey continued, taking another sip from the glass. "...But I'll need something better than a T-Shirt as a souvenir. Your wife drives a hard bargain, eh David?" She grinned.

Inexplicably, a sickening tightness gripped David's stomach, and he was suddenly slipping again.

His eyes were upon the food. His plate before him, half-cleaned. A cluster of chewed meat sat inside of his slack-jawed mouth.

Suddenly, the plate, previously holding all manner of savory, fresh food, changed.

The plate still held food, but it was replaced by rotting, maggot infested slop.

The cuts of meat; which *were* steaming slices of turkey, were now bloody, mangled pieces of flesh.

Fur clung to the meat; *rat fur.*

All at once, the flavors in his mouth soured.

The savory turkey changed to the gamey, bloody taste of rat. He could feel clusters of fur jammed in between his teeth, squeaking as chewed.

He felt his stomach quiver and cramp, about to toss up everything it had taken in. He spit the mouthful he still held onto the plate.

But in the next instance, for a split second, he was back.

Abbey was looking at him.

"Aw. Peter is saying hi. Good dog." She said, looking down at the ground by David's feet.

David felt a wet tongue lick the hand at his side and he turned to look.

The nightmare was back.

There was no dog.

What sat on the floor at David's feet and licked his hand, was a man.

A man, nude and hunched over on all fours. A dog collar was clipped around his neck and David could just make out the rust covered name; "Peter" scrawled onto it. The man had his eyes closed, tears of bliss leaking from the corners. He licked at David's hand, nestling his head into him and awaiting a scratch behind the ears.

David sucked in a gasp and fell backward in his chair, collapsing onto the ground. He screamed, crawling away from the dogman who watched him.

The man rolled his head sideways, looking a little hurt at the strange way his master was acting.

"Get away from me!" David cried, crawling backward on his hands.

Abbey sighed and stood up from her seat at the table.

"Ah fuck... I told you that the medicine was important, David." She spoke, almost scolding.

David's attention was brought to her, and he was petrified with what he saw.

Gone was the beautiful, youthful woman. In her place, was a witch.

Thinning, wispy, gray hair hung knotted from her head and swayed lazily over her wrinkled and sunken features. When she looked at David, she grinned, revealing a nearly toothless mouth. Her clothes were rags, barely covering her wrinkled form. Sagging breasts, speckled with liver spots, warts, and stray hairs, bobbed back and forth as she took slow steps toward David.

"Who the fuck are you?!" David demanded. "*What* the fuck are you?! Where's...Where's Abbey!?"

"Right in front of you." The witch replied. "Though, how she *really* exists. Not as you knew her."

He kept crawling backward, scrambling over broken bottles and dirty needles that littered the decrepit shack that had replaced his home.

He bumped into something, no, into *someone*.

He stopped, turning to see.

Another man, dirty and unwashed, rolled around on the ground, smiling and giggling. His eyes stared off into nothing as he rocked back and forth.

"Stay back!" David shouted at Abbey, as he scrambled to his feet.

His head was spinning. Lines of thought and questioning were all firing in his head simultaneously.

He finally landed on one.

"The medicine." He began. "What is it?!"

Abbey smiled. "It is everything you've ever wanted. Everything you've ever needed. Peace, fulfillment, paradise."

David scowled. His eyes found a length of metal pipe on the floor and he scooped it up, brandishing it at Abbey.

"English! No Bullshit! You tell me everything! Now!"

Abbey sighed and clasped her hands together.

"Poverty has always been a problem, David." She took a step closer to him, reaching into her pocket. "Throughout time people have suffered from it and have been offered no solution. But finally, it was given to us. Paradise, in the only place that matters; *our minds.*"

She withdrew a bottle of pills from her pocket and shook them next to her face, staring back at David. "We are worthless, forgotten trash on the bottom of society's boot. These pills make us whoever, whatever, and wherever we want to be."

David eyed her, not loosening his grip on the metal pipe. "What about you then, huh?" He demanded. "Why don't you take them?"

Abbey opened her arms, gesturing around the room of the filthy shack. "My paradise is here. A caretaker for the forgotten and lost. Do not fight it David. You are where you belong."

"Yeah? What if I don't think so? What if I feel like walking out that door right now?" David countered, gesturing to the door behind him with a flick of his head.

Abbey almost laughed. "And go where? To the world that hates you? Despises you? Would you rather be in the rain? Sheltered under a cardboard box? Or here; where you can be anything that you want to be? You are where you belong, and the only place that will take you."

He looked around, taking in the pitiful dwelling and the others like him that were scattered about like medicated dogs.

All around him were people, stuffed into corners under blankets and boxes. All blissful, all peaceful.

He looked at the pill bottle that Abbey still held.

"Come home, David." She said. "We miss you."

The pipe hit the ground, and David just stared.

II

In a room in a nondescript medical building, one man waited for his coworker to return. Splayed all across his desk were charts, percentages, and figures.

The door opened and his partner returned, bearing coffee.

"These numbers are fantastic." He told the other man as he took the outstretched cup of coffee. "Three single inner city communities being tested. All three of them have had over a sixty percent decrease in violent crime and drug use, and that number is expected to keep falling."

"Powerful stuff." The coffee man replied.

The man drank his coffee and shook his head. "Wait until it's rolled out nationwide. With results like these, this is going to change the world."

Even a Worm

He could hear it, coming right for him.

Footsteps were audible on the other side of the wall and he knew it was about to happen.

A hand swept over the top of his cubicle, knocking down all of the action figures he had carefully arranged.

He saw his face then, peering over the wall and wearing that stupid sneer.

"Hey, *Gay*. I've got a call. Keep your dolls on your side." Derek, his coworker, huffed. He scowled, before ultimately sitting back down and picking up the phone.

"My name is *Clay,* not *Gay.*" Clay heard himself weakly protest.

But Derek either didn't hear or didn't care, as no response came from the other side of the cubicle.

Clay sighed, picking up the scattered action figures and setting them on his desk. He stopped to admire one particular figure as he lifted it up.

It was that of a superhero; **Ultiman**.

The figure was adorned in a dark green costume, with muscles bulging at every centimeter under the paint. A bright blue "**UTM**" sat proudly at the center of his chest. A cape hung from his shoulders and his hands held his hips in a heroic pose.

Clay smiled.

Ultiman had always been his favorite, ever since he was a kid. He'd been no stranger to bullies his entire life, and in his daydreams, Ultiman was always there to ward off any evil-doer that would dare come after Clay.

He placed the other figurines along his desk and kept Ultiman, stuffing the figure into his pocket.

He looked at the clock that hung next to him and then into his empty coffee cup. He threw a glance around his limited field of vision.

The office was quiet, except for muffled chatter and the occasional cough or sneeze.

Everything was as it always was; dull, gray, and bathed in indifferent fluorescence from the humming lights above. Cubicle farms are always the same; incredibly explicit in their depressive nature.

He glanced over the screen in front of him. A spreadsheet of numbers and figures stared back. It hurt his eyes to look at.

He took off his glasses and rubbed the bridge of his nose. He yawned, and decided that coffee was a good idea after all.

He stood up and shuffled toward the other end of the room.

Reaching the break room, he crossed toward the coffee machine that hissed softly. Above the machine, there was a poster plastered onto one of the cupboards.

The poster; featuring a ring of people holding hands and in the middle of skydiving, was titled with one word: **TEAMWORK.**

Clay felt his eyes roll and felt the same way he always did when he was met with one of these "motivational posters"; *insulted.*

He didn't know what it was about corporate America that always yielded the same formula; drawing parallels to the most abstract things to **inspire** your farm of depressed worker bees.

"We're not skydivers. Teamwork isn't life or death here. If we don't work right, we don't go splat. If we fuck up, all that happens is some higher-up has to sweat a little more when he goes to the annual 'board meeting circle-jerk'."

He sipped his coffee, neglecting to sweeten it. He decided that he'd keep it just as he felt; especially bitter today.

He turned around and what he saw made him choke on his drink.

It was her; Melissa, the receptionist.

She was the sweetest, most amazing woman Clay had ever known, and he was quite certain; the most beautiful.

A nauseating but equally delightful pit opened in Clay's stomach, and he felt himself beginning to sweat. He swallowed, trying to suppress a cough that wanted to spew out the coffee he had choked on.

He reached into his pocket with his free hand and gripped Ultiman. He felt himself begin to center and calm down.

As ready as he'd ever be, he walked toward her.

"H-....Hi, Melissa." He started, hating how squeaky his voice sounded.

Melissa turned, pressing start on the microwave and letting her food cook behind her.

"Oh hi, Clay." She responded, offering a polite smile.

"Wish I had seen you at the movie the other night." Clay said. "It was a good one."

"Sorry about that. I've had to take care of my Mom this past week." Melissa replied, still wearing a smile that was friendly enough.

"Hey, no worries." Clay said. "How about tonight?"

He felt the question leave his mouth like a glob of drool. He could feel his face growing red and immediately felt embarrassed, wishing he hadn't opened his mouth at all.

"Shoot." Melissa sighed, feigning disappointment. "I can't tonight."

Clay mustered up his most charismatic smile and said, "You sure are making me work hard for this second date."

Melissa's eyes fluttered shut for a split second and a small groan escaped her lips. This was what she had hoped wouldn't happen. Clay was a nice enough guy, but she had worried he would get the wrong idea.

"That wasn't a date, Clay." She said calmly. "We ducked out of the rain and into a coffee shop, that's shelter."

The microwave beeped and Melissa whirled around, retrieving her cup of noodles. She moved toward the door, tossing back, "See you around!"

Clay, feeling like his heart was being swallowed by his large intestine, followed. "Let me take you somewhere nice sometime! It'll be a great-"

Clay was cut off as he collided with someone entering the break room. His coffee cup turned up and splashed the hot beverage down his white shirt.

"Hey, Claywad." Derek's voice immediately hissed. "Watch where you're going. This is a hundred dollar shirt."

Clay didn't answer, his attention was on his own shirt. He retrieved some napkins and began to wring out his ruined work attire.

Derek's eyes went to Clay and then back out the door to where Melissa had been.

"Were you bothering Melissa?" He asked. "I thought I told you to stay away from her."

Clay looked up from his shirt. His face was crimson and flecked with drops of coffee. "Now hold on, Derek. She's not yours t-"

Suddenly, Derek had him by the ruined shirt. He shoved Clay backward into the wall, pinning him there and pushing his face close to his.

"Stay. Away." He instructed, letting Clay go after another few seconds.

II

Clay sat in his car in the parking lot outside. Shirt ruined, and trying his best not to cry, he held the Ultiman figure in his hand.

He breathed rhythmically and exhaled slowly, attempting to calm himself. His gaze wandered upward toward the rear view mirror, and he locked eyes with Ultiman. No longer just a figure, but a living breathing person, sitting in his back seat.

Ultiman watched him with disappointed eyes.

Clay dropped his eyes, looking at the steering wheel instead.

"You let that prick walk all over you." Ultiman spoke.

"I can't do anything about him." Clay replied. "He's my coworker."

"That doesn't matter." Ultiman said. "What do I always say?"

Clay lowered his head even more.

"What do I always say?" Ultiman pressed.

"There's never a wrong place to do what is right." Clay responded, his head still hung.

"Exactly!" Ultiman exclaimed, clapping Clay on the shoulder. "You need to start standing up for yourself Clay! You still didn't talk to Melissa."

Clay raised his eyes to the mirror again, meeting Ultiman's. "She doesn't even remember I exist."

"So make her!" Ultiman exclaimed. "Stand up straight, be confident!"

Clay whirled around to look at Ultiman directly. "That's easy for you to say! Your day job is a private investigator. I'm an accountant. I'm nobody."

"So be the best damn accountant anyone has ever seen." Ultiman replied. "Everyone has a-"

"Everyone has a battle to fight." Clay finished his slogan for him.

"Exactly." Ultiman nodded. "Now let's go get some food."

"I'm not hungry." Clay said with a shrug.

"Fine, beer." Ultiman countered. "Let's go somewhere instead of sulk."

III

They sat at a corner booth in a semi-crowded pub. Ultiman drank a beer and inspected the room. Clay picked sheepishly through a basket of fries in front of him.

"Ah!" Ultiman almost shouted, as he slammed the now empty beer glass down. "Just what the doctor ordered. How are the fries?"

"They're ok." Clay shrugged.

Ultiman furrowed his brow, looking at the fries and then to Clay. "They're shitty aren't they?"

"No, they're ok." Clay replied. "They're just fries."

Before Clay could stop him, Ultiman reached out and snatched a fry, popping it into his mouth. A moment later, he spat it out in disgust. "Oh God. They're cold as ice. Ask for new ones."

"No, really. I'm fine." Clay protested.

Ultiman lowered his head, sighing a little in frustration. "Jesus, Clay. If you can't stand up for yourself over some icy french fries, I don't know how you're ever gonna find the balls to talk to Melissa."

"Knock it off." Clay whined. "It's been a long day."

"Hold up." Ultiman interjected. "Speaking of Melissa..." He tilted his head sideways and jerked a thumb across the bar.

Clay turned, though he was almost afraid to.

His eyes found her; Melissa sitting alone at a booth and eating a sandwich.

"Now's your chance. Go for it." Ultiman instructed, giving Clay a clap on the arm.

"I don't know." Clay said, nervously.

"Oh, grow some balls." Ultiman scolded. "I don't see that Derek prick, it's your time to shine."

Clay breathed in deeply, trying to calm his fluttering heart. "Ok, I'll do it."

Just as Clay moved to sit up, Derek appeared at the booth from his right.

"Well, shit." Ultiman huffed.

"Hey, Claywad. You stalking us or something?" Derek asked. "I come out of the bathroom and catch you staring at my girl?"

"Leave me alone, Derek." Clay said, lowering his head.

Derek grinned, an idea forming behind his mocking eyes. "Hey, don't you know you're supposed to shower before you go somewhere nice? Here, I'll help you." Derek reached onto the table and plucked up one of the beers. Tilting it, he poured it over the top of Clay's head.

Clay gasped and shook his head as the cold liquid ran over his nose and mouth. It dripped from his hair and down the back of his shirt.

Derek laughed and put the empty glass back onto the table. "Leave. Us. Alone."

Clay shot up out of his chair and sprinted to the door. He could feel the heat of the embarrassment warming up his chilled flesh as he burst from the door and onto the street.

He caught a glimpse of Melissa in the corner of his eye as he left. She watched him, looking sad and piteous at the soaked man.

IV

Feeling defeated and totally miserable, Clay sat on the couch back in his apartment. His hair was still damp with beer. Dirty dishes lay across the coffee table in front of him.

Or they did, until Ultiman strode by and swept them from the table in a mighty crash.

"Enough is enough, Clay! I'm not standing by and letting him push you around anymore!" Ultiman shouted, his foot resting on the now empty coffee table.

"I wasn't even bothering him." Clay said hollowly, staring off into the distance. "I was minding my own business."

"Exactly!" Ultiman exclaimed. "He's a bully and a creep. You need to teach him a lesson."

"How?" Clay asked, looking back at Ultiman. "I can't just attack him. I work with him."

"Bullshit!" Ultiman clamored. "Did I wait for *The Jaguar* to break into my sanctum and attack?"

"Issue #24" Clay replied, knowingly.

"You're fucking a-right, issue #24! I went and beat the prick to a pulp inside of his own lair. I didn't wait. I saw what needed to be done, and I did it." Ultiman roared.

"But, you have superpowers." Clay said, shrinking back into the couch. "I can't beat up Derek. He's twice my size."

"You have a gun."

"What?" Clay asked, almost gasping. "...I've never even shot it. It's still in the case."

"So take it out of the case, and issue #24 his ass." Ultiman replied, as if it were the most obvious solution in the world.

"I don't know..." Clay said, trailing off and thinking quietly to himself.

"If you don't have the stones right now, we'll tie him up in the trunk until you do." Ultiman helped him up, grasping his hand and pulling him to his feet.

"Ok." Clay finally said.

After a moment, Clay walked to where it was.

Not the gun, that would come in time.

He first walked to his desk. A manila folder lay atop a stack of books. He opened it; a stack of files he'd brought home from work.

Payroll forms.

He flipped through the papers, tossing aside the ones that weren't needed. Finally, the name Derek Bilman stared back at him.

"A name just as ugly as the person that wore it." He thought.

He read the address.

67 Anwiel St. APT C

The city.

He would go tonight.

V

He sat in his car, parked down the block from the apartments.

The gun was stuffed into the pocket of the fleece jacket he wore, and the weight of it pushing against his side was almost arousing.

"You ready?" Ultiman asked, sitting at his side like a partner at a stakeout.

"Yeah." Clay spoke, confidently and unafraid.

He popped the door open and stepped out onto the damp asphalt outside. He crunched along loose gravel and broken glass. The door to Derek's apartment was in his sights.

He approached the stairs and took a moment to himself, before beginning the ascent.

He took the brass of the old, worn doorknob. In his hand, it felt almost electric, energizing him with its touch.

He was about to pull it open and walk inside, when a scream behind him stopped his advance.

He turned, confused and searching for where the noise had come from.

Some movement in an alleyway on the opposite side of the street caught his attention and he squinted, trying to make out what was going on.

A man was grappling with a woman in the alley. He had two hands on her purse and wrenched it back and forth, trying to pry it from her grasp.

Clay turned fully, and began to walk down the stairs. His hand caressed the pistol in his pocket, his palm sweating slightly on the grip.

"Clay?" Ultiman asked. "Where the hell are you going?"

"Standing up for someone like me." He replied, his voice firm and certain.

"Bad idea." Ultiman insisted. "Forget what I said. Let's go home."

Clay turned to Ultiman, meeting his gaze.

"There's never a wrong place to do what is right."

Without another word, he left the stairs and jumped down the curb.

He jogged across the street, moving after the man and woman that were disappearing further into the alley. The woman screamed again, and Clay quickened his pace.

Before he knew it, he was ducking under a fire escape and squeezing past a dumpster. Moving forward and disappearing into the darkness after them.

He came around a corner, ready to jerk his gun from his pocket and shout; "Let her go!"

But that didn't happen.

Around the corner, when he came into view of the two people, they were waiting for him.

The man held Clay at gunpoint, with the woman cackling at his side.

"Howdy, Mr. Hero." The man said, with a toothy grin. "Let's have your wallet."

Clay froze for a moment, then reached for his wallet to do as the man said.

"Uh-uh." The man said, making Clay stop just before his pocket. "Cherry will get it."

Cherry did.

She jumped from the man's side and walked up to Clay's back. She reached into his pocket and withdrew his wallet. She left Clay's side and returned to the man, counting the cash in the wallet as she did.

"Woo! I like the hero. He's got deep pockets." Cherry said with a snickering laugh.

"That true, Mr. Hero?" The man asked, smiling even wider. "How deep your pockets go?"

"That's all I have." Clay stammered out. "I swear."

"How about those pants?" The man asked. "They look nice, I could use a new pair."

Both Cherry and the man laughed at that. Howling, cackling laughter escaped them as they held Clay at gunpoint.

A sickening, putrid smell from a dumpster crossed Clay's nose, as he took in the humiliation from the muggers.

"No." He said, suddenly.

The grin vanished from the man's face instantly and he raised the gun up at Clay's head.

"What'd you say?" The man asked.

Clay swallowed. "I said 'NO'." He replied, even more collected. "Now, give me back my wallet."

The man laughed again. "Now, how do you picture me doing that?"

"One of two ways." Clay began, his voice only shaking a little. "You toss it to me and you two run along. Or I pick it off your corpses, and wipe your blood off of it."

They both laughed at that.

Suddenly, Clay reached for his gun and pulled.

But it was stuck, the sights were snagged on loose thread inside of his jacket pocket.

Before he could wrench it free, the sudden motion caused the man to react.

The gun went off in his hand and the bullet met Clay's skull.

Clay didn't even get a final word out before his brain exploded out of the back of his head. The gore painted the dumpster that had sickened him with its smell, only moments before.

The muggers looked down upon the dead man for a few moments, before scattering and disappearing into the night with a wallet full of cash.

When the paramedics found him later that night, one of them was particularly upset by a single detail.

In one of Clay's hands was a gun. In the other, a bloody action figure, gripped tightly under the dead fingers.

VI

In the office on Monday, Derek and Melissa sat at a table in the break room.

From the door came one of their coworkers; a middle aged man named Phil Henley.

Phil went to the fridge and retrieved a cup of yogurt, before coming to the table.

"Did you hear about that Clay guy over in accounting?" Phil asked.

"Yeah. We heard." Derek replied.

"Did you guys know him? I don't think I ever said more than two words to him." Phil inquired.

"We knew him." Derek said. "He seemed like a nice enough guy, but he definitely needed some mental help."

"Really?" Phil asked, licking the lid of his yogurt.

"The guy wouldn't stop following me." Melissa interjected. "To the breakroom...to the bathroom...It was getting scary.

"I finally tried to talk to him the other day." Derek continued. "Right over there." He pointed to the door of the break room.

"I bumped into him, coming in here. I accidentally made him spill his coffee. So, I got some napkins and helped clean him up. I told him I was sorry... But before I could say much else, he started yelling at me about Melissa. How she was his, and I was stealing her. So, I put my hands on his shoulders. I just wanted him to understand... He seemed so lost and out of it. I told him that he was scaring Melissa. I told him that maybe he should talk to the company counselor. I even offered to give him a ride if he needed it."

"Jesus." Phil sighed out.

"We saw him that night." Melissa spoke. "The night he died. Derek and I were out at dinner. Clay just appeared across the restaurant and kept staring at me. I lost my appetite, and Derek went to go talk to him again."

"What did he say?" Phil asked Derek.

"He didn't say anything that really made sense. He was pretty drunk. I told him he should probably cool it on the drinks and I tried to help him set down the beer he was drinking. He yanked it back and poured it all over himself. He ran out of there before I could do anything to help him." Derek finished.

"Poor guy." Phil sighed. "I have a nephew like that. Nice enough, but a little strange and not good at communicating."

He put a hand on Derek's shoulder.

"Well, don't beat yourself up too bad. Sounds like you were really cheering for the guy to turn it around." Phil said, before tossing his finished yogurt in the trash and walking out of the break room.

"I boxed up all of his action figures." Derek told Melissa. "I think we can send them to his family. I hope they're doing ok."

Finders Keepers

His wife was in the trunk of the car, rolled up into a rug.

The night was cold. Faint wisps of exhaust that billowed up from the tailpipe made the already horrific event all the more somber.

Grant looked up, throwing his gaze out over the city below. Gravel crunched under his feet where he stood; high up on the mountain at a rural overlook.

He sniffed in, fighting back tears.

The aroma of gas stung his nostrils and he looked down at the plastic container he held.

For a moment, he allowed his thoughts to drift over the past few days.

II

It had been a lazy Saturday. He and his wife Elise had been home, both with the day off. As often happens, with nothing to do and nowhere to go, board games were unboxed and played.

Grant smiled faintly as he remembered.

"You've fallen right into Hell-Avenue." Elise said, rubbing her hands together, sinisterly.

"You've got a hotel on every damn space. How does that even happen?" Grant asked, exasperated and holding the dice.

"Go on and roll." Elise chided. "I need a new Mercedes to match the Bentley."

Grant held the dice, looking over the cardboard spaces and doing the math in his head.

"I'm screwed no matter what I roll."

He looked up, meeting her eyes with a mischievous grin.

"There must be some *other* way I can pay to stay at your hotel madame..." He spoke in a soft, sultry voice.

"Hmmm. You'll still be about five hundred dollars short." Elise quipped back.

"Ooooh. Ouch."

"Just go on and roll, lover boy." Elise pressed, shaking her head and smiling.

Grant rolled and was met with two ones; snake eyes. He moved his little figure to the space and immediately handed over all of his money.

"There you are." He said with an exaggerated bow. "One shirt off my back."

"Thank you *very* much." Elise said as she sat back. Showing off, she counted through her money and offered a small, villainous chuckle.

The doorbell rang and Elise made no move to get up, seemingly not through showboating.

"I'll get it Rockefeller." Grant said, pushing his chair back and moving toward the front door.

"Ah, yes. Thank you Jeeves." Elise offered, complete with a snooty eyebrow raise.

Pulling open the front door, Grant was met with a delivery man, standing on the porch and holding a box.

Tufts of dirty blonde hair puffed out from under his work cap and a name tag that read; Dillon J., was pinned to his breast pocket.

Grant looked him over and thought that he had never seen a man look so tired.

"Package for you." Dillon said, offering the box to Grant.

"Who's it from?" Grant asked, taking the box and inspecting it.

"I don't know." Dillon replied with a shrug.

"Hey, Lise? Did you order something?" Grant called over his shoulder.

"Not that I recall." Her voice answered a moment later.

Grant handed the box back to Dillon. "I think you have the wrong house, I'm sorry."

Dillon lowered his eyes and quickly looked back and forth. "Hey man, between you and me... I'm on thin ice at work. If I don't get all my stops done today, I'm getting canned. Would you please just take it?"

Grant hesitated. "I don't know..."

Dillon sighed and thought for a second.

"Look, just sign here and toss it in the trash if you want." He held up a clipboard. "I just need to hand this in at the end of the day, with all of the signatures. I really need this job man..."

"Ok...I guess..." Grant relented and signed the clipboard.

"Thank you so much." Dillon said, breathing a sigh of relief.

"Uh, sure." Grant offered, taking the box. "Good luck with the job man."

He turned and set the box down inside. But when he stood back up, Dillon was already gone.

Grant stepped out onto the porch and looked up and down the road. When he didn't see the man anywhere, he shrugged and made his way back inside.

Elise was waiting for him, looking at the box on the ground.

"You just took it?" She asked.

"I didn't really get an option." Grant replied, shutting the door behind him. "Should we open it?"

"Well, yeah." Elise answered, eagerly curious and as if it was the most obvious question in the world.

Grant looked a little more closely at the package, stooping down to handle it.

It was a strange parcel.

No label or address information was on it. The cardboard was wrapped in brown shipping paper and bound with twine.

He fished his keys from his pocket and unfolded a small pocket knife that was attached to the ring. He slipped the blade below the tightly fastened twine. The rope popped and the shipping paper fell to the sides, revealing the cardboard underneath. Carefully, he pulled back the flaps and reached inside.

When his hands brought out a small wooden box, he was almost disappointed. He held it up to his ear and shook it.

"Empty?" Elise inquired.

"I think so." Grant replied, still fiddling with the thing. "Maybe it's just decorative, like an antique or something."

"Hmmm." Elise breathed, sounding a little underwhelmed.

Grant held the box up and traced the edge where the two sides met. A faint and rough wax seal was felt underneath his finger tip and he brought it up to his eyes, holding it to the light.

"Hang on." He said. "I think I can get it open."

He pressed the blade he held into the slit and slid the knife along the seal. A second later, and the box popped open with a 'woosh', as a visible wisp of steam shot out from the box.

"Jeez." Grant muttered. "Sealed air tight."

Elise didn't respond.

Grant looked up to her and saw with horror, that her eyes were rolling back in her head.

A sickening roll began to take over his stomach. Suddenly, he was met with memories of news articles. Ones about anthrax and other poison sent through the mail by maniacs.

How had he not thought of that before?

He dropped the empty box and grabbed Elise by the shoulders.

"Elise!" He shouted as he shook her. He felt his stomach drop another twenty feet as he sensed her convulsing in his grasp.

"Elise!" He yelled again. But she fell from his grip, collapsing onto the carpet; unconscious.

"Oh Jesus." Grant whimpered.

He leapt to her side and lowered his face above her mouth. Faint, warm breath met his cheek and he tried to remember what, if anything, he knew about CPR.

But he didn't need to do anything.

A moment later, Elise opened her eyes and began to sit up.

"Hey." Grant called, his heart thundering in his chest. "Are you ok?"

Elise looked around, her eyes foggy and confused.

"What happened?" She asked, dazedly.

"You passed out."

"I did?" She asked, trying to sit up more.

Grant slowed her, placing a hand on her chest. "Whoa, take it easy. Are you alright?"

Elise rubbed her head, still trying to get her bearings. "Yeah. I think that musty smell just got to me. I haven't eaten anything today either. You know how I get."

Grant *did* know that Elise was prone to faint if her blood sugar got too low. But he was not satisfied. "Do you need to go to the hospital?" He asked, worried.

"No. No, I'm fine. Let's just have something to eat." Elise assured him. She extended a hand to be helped to her feet.

Grant hesitated.

He picked up the box and smelled it himself. It did smell very musty and old, almost earthen. But it didn't smell noxious or poisonous, thank God.

Reluctantly, he decided to chalk it up to a horrible coincidence and took Elise' hand to help her up.

He guided her to the kitchen table, setting her down gently in a chair. Then, he retrieved the box, and promptly tossed it into the garbage can outside.

He wiped his hands off and returned to the kitchen to make his wife something to eat.

III

The day had passed without any other notable occurrences.

Elise felt shaky and weak. But she always did after a fainting episode.

Night had come, and he'd laid her down into the bed softly. She'd fallen asleep quickly and began to dream peacefully.

Grant watched her, a pit of nervous guilt still prevalent in his stomach. He kept his eyes on her, watching her chest rise and fall rhythmically.

He was certain he would not sleep tonight. But perhaps fifteen minutes later, he was snoring.

His eyes floated open some time later and he was looking toward the night stand. The clock stared back at him.

The time; 3:46, the numbers red and glaring.

He rolled over, extending an arm to embrace Elise. But his touch only met empty sheets.

An immediate cold crept up his spine and he was wide awake.

"Baby?" He asked in the sinister dark.

He kicked his legs free from the blankets that suddenly felt suffocating.

Jumping out of bed, he crept into the darkened hallway just outside.

"Elise? Where are you?" His words echoed off the walls and mocked him with their emptiness.

A creeping sense of being lost crossed into his mind and he felt he had never hated the night more.

He felt for the light switch and struck it, but the darkness did not go away.

He fiddled with the light some more, but the result was still the same.

He was left in crushing black, and his home; so familiar to him in the waking hours, felt foreign and surrounding.

Total darkness.

He fumbled back into the bedroom and returned to his nightstand. He opened the drawer and fished out a flashlight, flipping it on. His heart leapt a little when light came forth and the fear that he had felt drowning in a moment before, dissipated some.

"Elise?" He called, casting the yellow beam up and down the walls of the hallway.

The milky light met photos of family and friends and threw shadows in unfamiliar ways. The snapshots of faces on the walls seemed to scowl from behind their glass cages.

He reached the kitchen and could see that the door to the cellar was wide open. Cobwebs glinted in the light just beyond the door and he felt a shiver go through him.

Suddenly, he felt twelve years old again.

Afraid of the darkness and dingy basements that surely held monsters and demons most terrible.

He wanted to shut the door and look for Elise elsewhere, to ignore the most obvious solution. But he wouldn't allow it. He gulped down a mouthful of stringy saliva and marched meekly toward the cellar door.

He let out a breath before he crossed the threshold and thought for a split second he could see his breath.

Impossible.

The stairs creaked and cracked under him as he made his slow descent.

The stairs were old and wooden, with gaps in between. He tried his best to push out images of ghostly hands reaching from between the steps and clasping around his ankles, holding them in an icy grip. But try as he might, he could not take his eyes off of the stairs. Part of him thought for certain that a face would emerge, and if it did, he knew he would die of fright.

What may very well have been a full ten minutes later, he came to the end of the stairs. He breathed a sigh of relief and turned the corner, walking face first into a spiderweb.

A yelp that would have in any other circumstance been hilarious, escaped his throat. He immediately jumped out of his skin, sputtering and pawing at the tickling strands that clung to his face.

The web he decided must have been empty.

But that didn't stop his skin from insisting that something was indeed crawling over him. Wiggling and probing just under his collar... in his hair.

Then, he heard it. Heard her...

"In the food, in the chest, in the eyes..."

It was barely audible whispering. Mouthing of words that were given only the slightest push of air to cross the lips.

He spun his flashlight and saw her.

Elise was standing in the corner, head bowed and muttering.

Next to her, he saw the breaker box. It was open, with all of the switches turned off.

He rushed to her side.

"Honey?" He asked, grasping her shoulder and shaking her softly.

"*Time to go.*" Her lips mouthed.

"Elise!" He said, louder and shaking her harder.

This seemed to do the trick, as a moment later she was alert, though confused.

"Grant...?" She whispered softly.

"I'm here." He hugged her tightly.

"Where am I?" She asked.

"In the cellar." Grant said, releasing her. She seemed stable enough to let go of for a moment.

He turned to the breaker box and flipped all the switches back on, one at a time.

"The cellar?" Elise, asked.

A second later and she nodded, seeming to make sense of it.

"Are you ok?" Grant asked, shutting the breaker box and turning back to her. "You were muttering something to yourself and standing in the corner."

"I was?" Elise asked, her voice trailing off.

Grant reached up and pulled the string on a single bulb that hung from the cellar ceiling. The light came on and he extinguished the flashlight.

He held her shoulders and looked her in the eyes.

"Honey, are you sure you're feeling alright? I think we should go to the doctor, first thing in the morning."

Elise looked at him and nodded a little bit.

Grant took her arm and began to lead her back up the stairs.

IV

Morning came.

Sleep had been more elusive for Grant the second time around. But nonetheless, he snored as the sun filtered in between the blinds and warmed the bedroom.

Elise suddenly pounced onto the bed at his side, waking him with a start.

"Hey." She said with a grin, looking down at his startled expression.

"Hey." Grant offered, cautiously.

"I feel a lot better." Elise said with a calm smile.

Muscles that had been tensed for almost a full day relaxed inside of Grant. He breathed a sigh of relief.

"Really?" He asked. "That's great. I was really worried."

"Really." Elise assured him.

Grant raised a hand and brushed hair behind her ear. Elise leaned down and kissed him.

"I'm gonna make some breakfast." She began as she sat up from the kiss. "Should I make it a double?"

"Yeah." Grant replied. "I'm starving."

Elise narrowed her eyes playfully and gave him the hand signal for 'ok'.

"I'm gonna shower." Grant said, standing up. "I'll be right out."

"I'm not waiting." Elise said as she left, turning to wink. "Don't let it get too cold."

As Grant stood in the shower, he felt like fifty pounds had been lifted off of his shoulders. The water flowed down his hair and over his closed eyes. He could smell butter wafting in from out in the kitchen. He could hear Elise humming a song to herself.

All was well again and he exhaled as the warm water continued to run down.

He came out into the kitchen, wearing only jeans and drying his hair with a towel.

He came into view of Elise and the smell struck him as odd first. He could smell butter and pancakes, a very familiar smell. But there was some after-tone on the air that was foreign, perhaps chemical.

The *answer* to that mental question slapped him across the face, when he saw *what* Elise was adding to the batter; drain cleaner.

"What are you doing?" He asked, startled and staring.

Elise turned, looking confused. "Making pancakes?" She still held the drain cleaner in her hand and the soupy liquid was pouring into the batter.

"With Draino?" Grant asked.

Elise looked, and when she saw what her own hand was holding, she grew immediately as shocked as Grant.

"I...I grabbed vanilla. I swear." Elise half-whispered as she stared at the jug in her hand.

"That's it." Grant stated, and strode to Elise' side, taking the jug. "We're going to the hospital. Go get your shoes."

Elise shook her head, still lost in thought. "No. I'm fine. I had some weird dreams last night and I didn't sleep much. I'm sorry. I was just confused and out of it."

"Just out of it?" Grant exclaimed, raising his voice a little bit. "You're pouring poison into your food!"

He put the drain cleaner back under the sink and turned again to her. "You might have bumped your head when you fainted. We need to take you in. We need to get you an MRI or something."

"An MRI?" Elise shot back. "We can't afford that, Grant. Really, I'll be ok."

"I'm not asking, Lise, I'm telling. Go get your shoes and we're leaving in five minutes."

"NO!" Elise suddenly shouted. "I'm not going! You need to listen to me! I'm fine!"

Before Grant could respond, she stormed off. He could hear the bathroom door slam in the bedroom a second later.

He was left in silence and all he could do was silently think. He sighed and began to clean up the kitchen, pouring the poison batter down the drain.

V

Another day had passed and Elise had not spoken more than ten words to him. They didn't see each other much until bed.

They now laid apart from each other and any attempt from Grant to talk to her, was met with silence, or one-word answers.

His gut had turned something awful for hours, and he had finally fallen into an incredibly thin sleep.

He awoke, and this time when he found the bed empty, he felt annoyance first, rather than concern.

"Elise?" He asked, sitting up.

When no answer came, he sighed and retrieved the flashlight. The lights were cut again and when he saw the cellar door open, he knew where to find her.

This time he was not slowed by fear.

He marched across the kitchen and jogged down the stairs. When he reached the bottom, he was mid-sentence of; "Come back to bed, Lis-"

His words caught in his throat, like curdled milk and he gasped.

Elise was in her same spot, but sitting cross legged and facing him. Her eyes stared at him, but also through him. The whites were bloodshot and the pupils vacant.

Her arms were in front of her. One digging into the other with her nails, raking the flesh down and pouring blood.

"Elise!" Grant exclaimed and rushed toward her.

He scooped her up and carried her up the stairs. As he came into the kitchen, he was half-certain he heard a faint giggle come from her throat.

VI

He had raced to the hospital.

Elise sat mumbling in the passenger seat, her body flopping back and forth against the restraint of the seat belt.

They had arrived and Elise was whisked away. Taken back to have her arm stitched up and to be held for observation.

Grant had gone home in the morning to retrieve some fresh clothes for her when she was released.

Now, as he walked up the porch to his front door, he saw something taped to it; an envelope.

Flapping against its scotch tape mount, the envelope swayed lazily in the morning breeze. Grant stopped and peeled it off the door.

He examined it a moment, before opening it and sliding out the letter that was waiting inside.

The handwriting was scrawled and barely legible in some places and only a couple paragraphs long.

It read;

I'm so sorry. I thought that giving it to someone else would fix her. But it looks like I've just fucked us both. Not only did it not fix her, it all got worse. She's not going to get better and the box won't burn. I tried everything. But we're both leaving now so it won't matter.

I'm so sorry for what I did to you.

The Box.

Grant stood, staring at the sixty-six words and eight sentences. Over and over again he read it, hoping it would say something else, hoping it would say something crazy, something that he could easily dismiss. But, it didn't, and the sense it made to him chilled him to the bone.

It wasn't signed, and he racked his brain trying to remember the guy's name.

Dillon something... Dillon L. Dillon I. Dillon J!

Suddenly he was very certain that that had been it.

He went inside, going to his laptop and booting it up.

Social media was first.

He typed Dillon J. into the search bar. Several results popped up and he scanned over the profile pictures until he felt he had found it.

Dillon Jacks.

He closed social media and went to an internet search.

Dillon Jacks...

Several results auto populated and he felt his stomach drop.

Dillon Jacks Murder

Dillon Jacks Suicide

Dillon Jacks Motive

Dillon Jacks Wife

He clicked on the first news article that popped up on the following page, and began to read.

House fire in Crestwood found to be Murder-Suicide.

A house fire that was extinguished late last night in Crestwood, has now been ruled as a murder-suicide, after bullet casings were recovered and gunshot wounds were found on the remains of the two victims.

*Authorities now believe that Dillon Jacks: 29,
murdered his wife Carla Jacks: 27, before setting his house
ablaze and taking his own life.*

*Potential motives as of now are not yet clear, but the
authorities are pursuing all possible leads.*

*This story will be updated as more information
becomes available.*

Grant looked up from the page and saw that he
was trembling badly.

A few morbid timelines and some grim math
crossed his mind.

*If Dillon did this last night, he put the note on my
door yesterday.*

*I probably walked right by it taking Elise to the
hospital.*

In the panic, I must have missed it.

He was on my front porch sometime yesterday...

A million ideas and strange conclusions raced
through his mind, but they all landed in one area.

The box.

Dillon wrote that it wouldn't burn.

But that's crazy.

Anything that's wood, will burn.

So go try it.

No, this is all nonsense.

Is it? What are you afraid of?

I'm not afraid.

Yes, you are. Because if that box doesn't burn, then Dillon wasn't crazy.

That was that, and Grant stood from the chair, determined to find out one way or another.

He had thrown the box in the trash can, outside. But garbage day hadn't come, and it would still be in there.

He went outside and rounded the side of the house. Any thoughts he was currently having, crashed into themselves at ninety miles an hour, when he saw it.

The box was sitting on top of the garbage can.

Though he had covered it in many other bags of trash in the day or two it had been; (He couldn't readily recall exactly how many days it had been.) here it was, all the same.

The box sat, waiting for him. Almost looking him in the eyes and saying; "Remember me?"

The impossibility of the box's resting place was not something he wanted to consider right now.

He scooped it up, angrily and a little fearful... and brought it into the backyard.

He threw it onto the barbecue, dousing it with lighter fluid until the bottle was empty. When the metal container sputtered and crinkled up, he tossed it aside with a dull clang. He struck a match and held it to the box.

The fuel went up in a spectacular fireball, nearly taking his hair and eyebrows with it. He squinted and turned away from the flame. But when he turned back, there was the box, without so much as an ember growing on it.

The old antique box stared out from its crown of fire and did not even darken a shade.

He watched it for a while, hoping that somehow the wood might spontaneously combust. But the flames continued until they died around it. Giving up, as if they had been commanded to burn stone.

He hung his head as the final flames winked out.

When he returned inside, he collapsed onto the couch just as his phone began to ring. He reached into his pocket, bringing out the cell and reading the screen.

The incoming call read; **Western Valley Medical Center.**

"Hello?" Grant answered.

"Mr. Bridges?" A voice on the other end asked.

"Speaking."

"Your wife is in stable condition and ready to be picked up. The doctor *does* recommend that she stay the night for observation. Though I'm not seeing any insurance information on file."

"No." Grant said, rubbing his eyes and shaking his head. "I'll pick her up. Be there soon…"

He hung up.

He sat there for a while, thinking quietly over everything before packing up some clothes for Elise and leaving.

VII

He'd gotten to the hospital and pulled to the front. Elise and a nurse were already outside, waiting for him.

Elise sat in a wheelchair, her head hung low. The nurse passed her off and vanished back inside before Grant could even say two words to her.

They were outside the house now, parked in the driveway and sitting in silence.

"Grant." Elise spoke, softly and for the first time since he had picked her up.

Grant turned to her, meeting her tear-streaked and bloodshot eyes.

"Grant, I don't know what's happening to me..."

Her voice broke and more tears began to fall from her parched eyes. "I feel like I'm falling apart. Ever since we opened that box, I haven't felt right... I don't know what to do." She sniffed.

Grant decided not to mention all that he knew now. After all, what good could it really do?

He simply embraced her, gripping her shoulders tight and not wanting to let go.

"I love you." Elise sobbed out. "You know that right? I love you so much, baby."

"I know." Grant said, gingerly. He took her head and pressed it against his chest, stroking her hair softly. "I love you too."

VIII

Sometime during the night, Grant woke up.

He didn't turn to see if Elise was still in bed, he knew that she wouldn't be. Instead, he stared at the ceiling, tracing his eyes over the rough moulding.

He sighed, bitterly.

There was an emptiness in his chest and heart that hurt to focus on, but it was impossible to ignore. He wanted to cry, wanted to scream, but no tears would come. He felt like he was stuck halfway into a sneeze and the actual feeling was just as enjoyable.

Pain, searing pain.

Grant reached toward his shoulder where the sudden, shooting pain was. But Elise grabbed his wrist and climbed on top of him before he could do anything.

Stabbed. I've been stabbed. But, with what? I hid all of the knives.

He fought against Elise who twisted the sharp object in his shoulder. The corner of his vision caught what was sticking into him and he knew.

Bristles of a toothbrush were clenched between Elise's fingers, as she twisted and worked the sharpened end under his shoulder.

He wanted to lay back and let her do it, to let her cut his throat. Let her gouge out his eyes, or whatever it was she was going to do. But that damned survival instinct took over and he fought back.

He gripped her fist in his own, and felt a sickening shift of malleable plastic bending around his ligaments and tendons.

"Don't fight." Elise spoke, suddenly. Her voice was distorted, almost as if it were joined by several voices behind her own. "Don't fight, sweetie. I love you."

Adrenaline coursed through Grant's veins and he roared. "Get off me!"

He used her own weight against her and heaved her sideways. The force launched her high through the air and she crashed into the wall with a mighty boom. The sheetrock crunched beneath the force and left a body-sized dent in the wall.

Elise fell to the ground in a heap, but was back up a second later, charging at Grant with the toothbrush still in her grasp.

Grant was up now, facing her. He lifted his foot and caught her in the stomach, pitching her up and over him.

This time she sailed over the bed completely and landed on her head, awkwardly.

He heard an audible, sickening crunch as her neck broke and she lay still on the floor.

"Elise...?" Grant asked the quiet room.

He stood and walked around, falling to her side. She lay in a heap and Grant rolled her over, tenderly. Sickened with himself, he raised his fingers to her neck and checked for a pulse.

Dead.

He cringed away from her body, not wanting to believe it. He pushed himself into the side of the bed and grasped his temples, beginning to sob hysterically.

Before he could mourn a second longer, Elise's neck snapped sideways and she was staring at him with white and milky cataracts that covered her pupils.

"*Hello. Loverboy.*" The thing that wore Elise' face spoke from its crippled throat.

It tried to move, to crawl and attack him again. But its broken and paralyzed body refused to obey its commands.

It roared in frustration and hissed at Grant.

"You let her go! You let Elise go!" Grant shouted at the thing.

A deep, guttural laugh bellowed hoarsely from the thing's bowels.

"She's in Hell. They're raping her pretty little soul as we speak." The demon's voice spoke. *"That soft, beautiful flesh..."* The thing sniffed in, groaning in ecstasy. *"Ripe for suffering."*

"Shut up! Shut up!" Grant shouted at the thing as it laughed.

He grabbed a sock that was discarded on the floor and stuffed it into the thing's mouth, trying to silence it. It caught one of his fingers on the way out and bit down, severing it.

Grant felt his stomach leap as the bone in his finger snapped like a baby carrot. Blood spewed from the stump on his hand and he withdrew it back in pain, as the thing's muffled laughs continued. His mutilated finger fell from the mouth and rolled onto the carpet.

"Fuck you!" Grant shouted and kicked the thing in the face.

The monster did not stop, did not quiet.

It laughed and cackled behind the sock in its throat as black bile began to weep out around it.

Grant gripped his head and felt that he would surely go mad. But one single word crossed his mind and he knew what he must do.

Fire.

IX

Grant pulled himself out of his head and away from the terrible memories within.

He heard the thing move slightly in the trunk and he moved to pick up the gas can.

He'd bound up the creature in blankets, towels, a rug, and ropes. He'd drug it down the stairs of his porch and into his car.

He thought that if any of his neighbors had been peering out of their windows then, that they'd gotten quite the scene.

But it didn't matter now.

He uncapped the gas can and poured it all over his car. He opened the doors and splashed it inside too.

He stepped back and set a box of matches on the roof.

He took a deep breath and raised the can above his head, pouring the fuel over himself.

He looked down from the mountain overlook and remembered the first time they'd come here; on their first date.

He sighed, and struck the match.

X

After a couple weeks of investigation, and after all of the evidence had been collected from Grant and Elise's house, the property had gone up for auction.

Along with the house, several other items were on the list for sale.

Among them, a small, wooden, antique box, sealed with wax.

Echoes of a Fever Dream

You've always hated to throw up.

Ever since you were little and sick for the first time, that nauseating feeling of curdling bile frightened you more than the actual act of vomiting.

You could feel it coming on as the fever made you perspire hotly, complimenting the sweat that wept from your saliva glands in your mouth.

You would cry out, calling for your parents.

Sometimes they would rush to your side, offering you a vomit bowl or ushering you to the toilet. Other times, you were left alone, calling out in the dark and too weak to get to the light.

Left alone in the black, sickly and afraid.

You feel it now; a pounding rushing in your ears as the fever fills your head with static.

Your stomach curdles and you feel cold, so very cold.

You sit up, but you are no child anymore.

You are alone, solitary in your room. Half drunk glasses of water and bottles of pills decorate your nightstand.

There is no one to call for. No one is there to flip on the light.

You feel dizzy, feel weak.

Every inch of your body feels like it has its own personal heartbeat and your skin hurts to the touch.

Your closet is open and you see, only for a split second, a grim face staring out at you from behind the rows of hanging clothes.

Another second and it is gone.

Your eyes are fuzzy and you assure yourself that what you just saw was merely a spill, an overflow from the nightmarish land of fever dreams.

Or maybe not.

Another part of your hazy mind wonders for just a moment, if you might have just come very close to finding out what *actually* lurks in those places we don't dare look.

You think that you might have just seen something you were not supposed to see.

You sit alone in the dark, only able to wait and find out.

The Memory Box

There is nothing in the world that brings sudden clarity more than a punch to the nose.

Cole Clark found that clarity about five seconds after the initial punch, when he had rolled to the first floor landing at the bottom of the stairs.

He'd come home early, and had found his girlfriend with another man.

His girlfriend had been on the couch, naked. The man was in the bathroom but his clothes and shoes were on the floor near the couch.

Cole had yelled and shouted as is to be expected, and prepared to beat the ever-living shit out of the man.

That is, until he saw the sheer size of the roid-battered monster that emerged from the bathroom.

He immediately knew the fight wouldn't be much of a fight. But he was determined to get at least one good lick in. He balled up his fist and struck the man in the jaw.

It was almost comical, the way the blow bounced off the man's face, like a BB gun fired at a steel wall.

He absorbed the blow and turned to Cole, who immediately regretted being so brave. The man grabbed Cole by the back of the shirt and dragged him backward toward the still open door.

Cole tried to think of something to say, but a blow to his nose shut down any quip that may have come.

It was surreal. As he tumbled down the stairs he could tell the guy hadn't broken his nose and he felt at least a little bit grateful for that.

Now as he sat down on the cracked concrete, with his few possessions and clothes raining down around him, he took a mental inventory.

The apartment was in his girlfriend's name and his own bank account had an impressive balance of -$32.67, (Courtesy of an eight dollar pack of beer and a

$24 'fuck-you' fee from the bank). He knew he would have to call a friend or sleep on the street.

One name came up in his mind, or rather a nickname; Squishy Reynolds.

He'd been friends with Squishy since elementary school. But he hadn't talked to him much in the years following highschool.

Squishy was an alright guy and a decent friend, but he ran drugs, and not just weed.

Squishy's real name was Seth, but he had been known as Squishy ever since the fifth grade. Cole could barely remember now where the nickname had come from. But it was a relatively simple story, as most nickname origins are.

Once in the fifth grade, Squishy's Grandmother had been visiting. Cole, Squishy, and several of their other friends were at the house, and were on their way out.

Squishy's Mom halted his exit and made him give his Grandmother a hug and kiss before he left. A fact that made the other boys giggle as Squishy glared at them.

Morosely, Squishy had meandered to his Grandmother's side and half-heartedly thrown his arms around her.

"Seth... my goodness. You're so squishy." His Grandmother had said as she embraced him.

Apparently, Seth had put on a bit of weight since his Grandmother's last visit and she had taken notice.

The other boys erupted into laughter and Squishy Reynolds was born.

His job these days, while a very risky and dangerous business, was usually very dull. It typically consisted of driving to one spot, picking up a dead-drop, and driving it to another spot.

No harm, no foul.

But the potential was always there for either violence from a rival, or extensive prison time. As such, Cole had grown apart from Squishy, mostly from the insistence of his girlfriend.

The door slammed behind Cole and he came out of the thought. He reached into his pocket and withdrew his phone, scrolling through to find Squishy's number.

He found it, and dialed.

As the phone rang, Cole drummed up an apology in his head. It had been at least a few years since he'd talked to Squishy, and he owed him at least a 'sorry'.

But as he heard the line connect and Squishy's voice come through, he realized he'd been worried for nothing.

"Cole!" Squishy's voice came through the speaker, his voice excited. "It's been too long brother! How are you doing?"

A pang of guilt hit Cole in the chest and he felt like a real dick. Here he was calling a friend who clearly missed him, only to ask for a place to stay.

"Hey, Squishy." Cole replied, grinning on the other end of the phone call. "I'm doing fine, just living the dream... How about you?"

"I'm good, brother. Wanna come by? I'm still at the same spot."

Cole breathed in, taking a second before asking. "Yeah, that'd be great. Hey... you think I might crash on your couch a couple nights? Just a temporary thing of course."

"Trouble with Dina?" Squishy asked.

"Yeah, something like that." Cole replied, looking back up the stairs to his old front door.

He felt something warm drip onto his hand and he looked down. His nose was bleeding, and pretty badly. His mouth, chin and neck were covered, along with the entire front of his shirt. He looked like a maniac, drenched in blood and sitting on the sidewalk around crumpled up clothes.

"Hey, no problem. *Mi casa es su casa*, brother." Squishy continued. "You swinging by now?"

"Yeah." Cole replied. "If that's alright."

It was.

Cole said goodbye and ended the call. He stood up and began to gather everything he could carry from the sidewalk.

As he scooped up a shirt and balled it up, something metal jingled to the concrete. He looked down and saw what it was.

The mail key.

He looked up at the door again; still locked and shut.

He picked up the mail key and kept it, as he walked to his car that was still parked out on the street.

As he loaded up his trunk, he tossed the key into a storm drain at the end of the gutter.

An immature, little 'fuck-you', that even Cole knew was pretty dumb.

II

Two months passed, and Cole, without any other avenues to pursue, began to work for Squishy.

First, he was only a ride along, lending a hand and an extra set of eyes for lookout when needed.

But after many successful drops, Cole started to be offered work. The money became better and he was able to move out and get an apartment of his own; an idea that seemed like a distant pipe dream only a month ago.

The work still made him nervous, and he would always clench his ass a little tighter when the odd police cruiser would pull behind him on the road.

But he had never run into any trouble, yet.

It was seven in the morning when he got the call.

He sat up in bed. His head throbbed dully as it approached the full strength of the hangover that awaited. He reached to the nightstand and plucked up the yammering phone, squinting as the screen lit up.

"Hello?" He asked, rubbing his eyes.

"Cole." Squishy's voice said on the other end.

"Yeah?" He replied, his voice hoarse with sleep.

"We've got a job we need you on." Squishy said in his professional voice, that was a stark contrast from his normally friendly and laid back tone.

"Right." Cole replied, sitting up and retrieving his shoes. He pinned the phone between his ear and shoulder as he stooped to hop into a pair of pants.

"5th and Grant?" He asked, reciting the usual spot.

"No. No, this one's different." Squishy replied.

Cole's interest piqued. "Different?"

"Yeah. It's a mountain road, I'll send you a GPS ping." Squishy continued. "You'll need a shovel too."

A shovel? This one really is different.

"Can I ask what's going on?" Cole questioned.

"Sure, why not." Squishy replied. "We had a cook working up in a camper in the mountains. He had to dip out fast and he buried the stash. You need to dig it up and bring it back. I'll ping the drop location too."

"Crank then?" Cole asked, a little disappointed.

Out of all the junk he ran, meth was the only one that made him uneasy. It wasn't any more dangerous than running anything else, besides weed. But images of toothless and scabby-faced people from anti-drug programs growing up always crossed his mind.

"Yup." Squishy answered. "How soon can you get going?"

"I'm going now."

III

He swung his car around another bend and heard the shovel rolling around in the back. It was clanging into the sides of the car and making a racket that was starting to get on his nerves.

He glanced down at the phone between his legs and tried to make out if he was getting closer or further away from the coordinates.

He was driving on a one lane dirt road that stretched up and around the mountains.

Trees surrounded him on both sides and it was incredibly disorienting. He'd had to double back twice already and one more was going to be way too suspicious for his liking.

He scanned the trees and by some miracle, he finally saw a puny and rocky path that led further into the woods. He slowed down, gripping the wheel tightly as the vehicle began to buck and shake as it was led off of the road.

He continued down the hidden road another mile, flicking his eyes to the gps intermittently. The signal was bad already and the thick forest seemed to make it even worse the deeper he got.

When it looked like he was right on top of it, he stopped the car and got out. He walked around to the trunk and opened it, retrieving the shovel.

He had just bought it at a hardware store on the way out here and a label was still zip tied to the handle.

It was still usable with the tag attached, but it would definitely get annoying.

He realized he had no idea how deep this stash would be and didn't want to have a zip tie tearing up his hand with every shovelful he dug.

He tugged at the plastic tie, trying to remove it.

The plastic was thick and dug into his skin as he tried to snap it with brute force. When it wouldn't budge, he pulled his stinging fingers away and reached into a small case that was next to the shovel.

It was a roadside utility kit, filled with an assortment of things that would be useful in a pinch. He rifled through it and found what he was looking for; a small, gray pocket knife.

He slipped the blade underneath the zip tie and popped it easily. Casting the label from the shovel, he folded the knife up and put it into his pocket.

He reached up, gripping the trunk and shutting it.

As he stood silently in the clearing now, he could hear just how full of life the forest was. Birds chittered high up in the trees and warm sunlight filtered through the branches. A small creek babbled somewhere off to the left and the smell of the forest was a sweet and earthy aroma. Fall was on its way and some leaves had begun to grow auburn, but Summer hadn't fully given up yet.

Aside from what he was actually doing out here, this wasn't a bad place to spend such a beautiful day.

He brought his phone back out of his pocket and zoomed in. The reception was horrendous and half of the map wouldn't fully load. But it looked to him as if he was standing maybe twenty or thirty feet from the ping.

He holstered the phone again and slung the shovel against his shoulder. In a growing circle, he began to walk and scan his eyes over the ground.

He stepped around, going in loops for what seemed like ten minutes. Now and then, he would consult the gps again. Though, the delay from the poor service was so bad, that the map would only update about once every thirty seconds.

Sometimes, it would say that he was standing right on top of it, and then it would update and jump his location to fifty feet past it.

Growing increasingly frustrated, he considered marching back out to the road and calling Squishy to tell him what a shit show finding the spot was.

To hell with the job. He was looking ridiculously suspicious to anyone who might happen to meander by.

But then, he saw it.

There was a large rectangular section of loose dirt, about the size of a kitchen table. It was so incredibly obvious in its presentation, that he didn't know how he had missed it before.

He also considered how poorly the cook had hidden the stash. The hole was filled in. But nothing covered it and anybody who looked at it for more than five seconds would guess that something had been buried there.

He sighed and stepped over it, beginning to get to work.

About five inches down, the task quickly became a chore. Under the loose dirt, a two inch thick layer of gravel revealed itself. The shovel grinded and squeaked loudly with each thrust and Cole worried about any passing hikers that might feel like investigating such a strange sound.

Another fifteen minutes and his back was screaming, as sweat poured down his face. His clothes were becoming soaked and the previously warm day became chilly as a loose breeze blew against his wet body.

THUNK.

He froze, taking a moment to internally register the sound. He lifted the shovel again and tapped it around where he had just struck.

THUNK.

THUNK.

THUNK.

"Oh, thank God." Cole exhaled, standing up to stretch his back out. "There you are, you bastard."

Though he had finally found it, it still took him over half an hour to uncover the lid completely. When the final handful of dirt was brushed aside, he collapsed against the side of the hole, wheezing.

The buried chest was an old, wooden trunk. It looked like something that might be for sale in an antique shop.

"Not waterproof and not very sturdy." Cole thought.

He decided that he'd give Squishy an earful about whoever this cook was and all of his bright ideas. If this guy was always working with them, he wasn't smart enough to be.

He finally caught his breath and stood up, dusting the dirt from his jeans.

He was filthy, covered head to toe in dirt.

If he was going to drive a trunk worth of meth out of the sticks, he was going to be waiting until night. He wasn't going to pull up to a stoplight looking like he'd just crawled from the earth, only to turn his head and see Officer Friendly staring him down.

What a big pain in the ass this day had turned out to be.

He stepped sideways and crouched, reaching along the side of the chest and feeling for a latch. When he found it, and had pried it loose, he threw the lid open with a heave.

The smell hit him before his eyes could see what was inside, and he recoiled back almost immediately.

When he had composed himself and looked back inside, he had to choke back a scream.

There was no meth, no drugs, no guns, nothing that Cole would be sent out here to retrieve.

Inside the box, there was only a dead girl.

She was maybe fourteen or fifteen years old. Cole had to guess on the age and he only picked 'teenager' because of the braces that clung to the yellowed teeth yawning out of her blackened mouth. Ants crawled through her vacant eyes, filtering out through her nostrils. He could see other bugs moving and wiggling under the sheet she was wrapped in, and he thought he might vomit.

He did.

He held his stomach, spitting bile out from his mouth, and was grateful that he had had at least enough time to move away from the coffin before he puked.

A stick broke somewhere above him and his attention whipped upward, bringing him face to face with a man.

A park ranger, standing on the dirt road he had taken out here.

Cole's heart jumped in his chest as he stared at the man. But when he remembered there weren't *actually* any drugs here, and he hadn't killed anyone, he calmed down. There was going to be a hell of a lot of explaining to do, but he should be able to make it out okay.

All he'd actually done was dig up the wrong hole.

"You okay pal?" The Park Ranger asked.

"Yeah. Just got sick." Cole said, realizing the man couldn't see inside of the box yet from where he was standing.

"What's in the hole?" The Park Ranger asked, walking closer and stretching his neck up to look.

"A dead body." Cole replied, still hunched on the ground. "Believe me, I'm just as surprised as you are."

The ranger looked wide-eyed and walked over to the hole, peering in.

His face grew sour and pale, he scowled. Unbeknownst to Cole, he withdrew his pistol.

"Hands on your head." The ranger spoke from behind Cole. "Now."

Cole turned around, quickly. "Hey man. I didn't do it! I just found her!" He was stammering and beginning to panic a little bit.

"Sure." The ranger replied, his gun still aimed at Cole.

"I swear to God! Bring the cops up here! Forensics... I don't know! I've never seen that girl before in my life!"

"That's just what I'm going to do." The ranger said.

He reached down with one hand, still holding the pistol with the other. He reached into his belt and withdrew a set of zip-tie handcuffs. He threw them at Cole's feet. "Put those on. We're gonna walk back to my cabin, and I'm going to radio the station."

"Hey man, come on." Cole protested. "You've gotta believe me."

The ranger returned both hands to the pistol. "If you're telling the truth, you've got nothing to worry about. Put on the cuffs and come with me. The police will figure out just what the hell is going on."

Cole sighed and reached slowly for the cuffs, keeping an eye on the barrel of the gun. He put them over his wrists and tightened them as much as he could with the limited leverage.

The ranger reached down and cinched it together tighter, and Cole winced as the thick plastic dug into his flesh.

"On your feet." The ranger instructed. He holstered his pistol and yanked Cole up by the wrists.

Cole stumbled over a rock and nearly went down, but the ranger caught him and pushed him forward.

He looked up, a little puzzled. The direction he was being led wasn't back toward the main road. He was instead being pushed deeper into the woods. A pang of concern flashed in his stomach and he tilted his head around.

"Where are we going?" He asked the ranger behind him.

"To my cabin. This is a shortcut." The ranger replied, not offering any further information.

Without much of a choice in the matter, Cole continued forward at the guidance of the man.

Five minutes passed and the ranger spoke again.

"Do you know who that was?"

"Huh?" Cole called back, confused.

"That girl."

Cole shook his head. "I told you. I just found her-"

The ranger cut him off. "That was Linda Terrance. She's been missing for three weeks now, along with a couple other girls. Your bullshit story... We'll have to see what the police say... But it's all very *interesting*."

"You've got the wrong idea. Call the cops, do whatever you have to do. I'm not your guy." Cole protested as he marched.

"We'll see." The ranger muttered.

They walked on. Over fallen logs and dried creek beds.

Twice, Cole fell on his face and the ranger had to help him up.

On the second occurrence however, Cole discreetly retrieved his pocket knife, tightly gripping it between his bound hands.

It was crazy, and probably a bad idea, but this man had a strangeness to him that Cole didn't particularly like.

If need be, he'd toss the pocket knife aside when he needed to. But until then, holding onto it made him feel better.

After perhaps another half mile, the ranger instructed him to turn left around a large tree.

Cole did as he asked and immediately froze.

There was no more path, and no cabin in sight. Instead, there was only a dead end. An embankment of dirt, climbing upward like a wedge. Thick brush and trees obscured the end of the crevice, and Cole felt his heart thunk into his stomach.

"On your knees." The ranger said, coldly.

"I... I didn't do anything." Cole protested, weakly.

"On your knees." The ranger repeated.

Dully, Cole eased down to his knees.

He could feel the ranger right behind him. Any moment now, he thought he would feel the cold metal of the gun being pressed into his skull.

"That girl didn't deserve to die. It didn't *need* to happen." The ranger spoke.

Cole gulped.

"But, she just wouldn't stop screaming."

The last sentence barely occurred to Cole, as he had been steadily sawing at the zipties ever since they had stopped.

The handcuffs snapped and he moved in one motion, cutting the knife sideways and backward, driving it into one of the ranger's calves.

The man screamed and the gun went off.

Cole felt a bullet whizz right by his ear and dirt exploded from the ground where the shot had landed.

He wasted no time. Jumping to his feet, he tackled the ranger to the ground.

In the commotion, the gun went off again, but embedded itself harmlessly into a tree, thirty yards away.

Cole batted away the gun and sent it flying to the dirt.

In another instant, he was on top of the ranger. Straddling the man, he rained down blows upon his head and face.

The ranger fought back weakly, raising his hands and arms to shield himself from the strikes.

Cole's eyes caught the gun to his side and he jumped off, reaching for it.

He felt fingers grasp his leg behind him and he lashed out a savage hit with his foot. The heel of his boot connected and he felt the cartilage and bone of the ranger's nose mash beneath it.

The man let go and rolled backward, clutching at his smashed face.

Cole's hands closed around the pistol and he crawled away, spinning to aim the weapon at the man.

"Wait!" The ranger shouted, sputtering on the blood that was pouring into his mouth. "Wait! If this is about your drugs... they're in a locker at my cabin. You can have them! They're all yours!"

Cole eyed the man, keeping the pistol trained on him, steadily.

"And!" The ranger exclaimed. "And... If you kill me... They'll never find the other bodies!"

Cole's finger tickled the trigger, wanting to squeeze it and send this psychopath to the grave that had been meant for him.

But his mind returned to the girl in the hole.

Someone's baby, someone's world, tossed into the ground to rot like trash. He wanted to squeeze the trigger even more as he thought about it, but he couldn't.

He eased his grip on the weapon.

Cole looked down and saw that the knife was still sticking out from the ranger's leg.

"Take the knife out and throw it to me." He said, coldly.

"What?"

"The knife." Cole continued. "Take it out of your leg. Then, throw it over here."

The man hesitated, struggling to look down at the wound. He sat up painfully and gingerly placed his fingers around the blade's handle. He yelped as he pulled it free and more blood squelched out from the hole.

The man looked at the knife and then to Cole.

He seemed to be judging his ability to throw it accurately enough to kill or wound. But as he looked into Cole's eyes, he knew that even thinking about trying that would mean death.

He tossed the knife underhand and it landed next to Cole's feet.

"Now." Cole instructed, sitting up. "Take out one of those zip ties and put them on."

Fire briefly flashed in the ranger's eyes. "Who the hell do you thin-"

He started to speak but shut up when Cole fired a round into his kneecap.

The ranger bucked and shrieked, clutching at the bullet hole and the shattered remains of the joint. He howled, rolling around in agony.

"Handcuffs!" Cole shouted.

After a moment, the man composed himself as much as he could and did as he said.

"Now, put one above your knee. You're not going to bleed out." Cole instructed.

The man's eyes grew even wider. But after several minutes of slow moving and pained motion, he had placed a zip tie just above his knee.

Cole approached, cautiously.

In two quick movements, he cinched up both zip ties tightly. Ignoring the man's screams, he stuffed the pistol into his waistband and grabbed the ranger by the collar.

It took almost an hour, but Cole eventually managed to drag the ranger to his car.

The ranger, who was slipping in and out of consciousness, could not do much to protest. When he reached the car, Cole popped the trunk and rolled the man into it.

He backed his car out.

Winding around, he turned back down the dirt path that led to the main road.

He watched his phone carefully, and when enough service was indicated by the bars, he dialed.

"I'm a few miles up Lawrence Mountain Road. I've found a dead body, and I have the man that did it."

IV

When the investigation had finally concluded after several weeks, and Cole himself was released from jail, there were indeed *many* bodies.

For *decades,* a serial killer, with a day job as a park ranger, had been active. With an extensive knowledge of the miles of woods and country, he would wait for the opportunity to arise and would strike.

Lurking outside of campers' tents in the dead of night and following hikers into the deep forest, he had had many opportunities.

Dogs were brought out to search the surrounding miles of country and in the end; 27 bodies were recovered.

The ranger was aging, and recently when he'd had a new victim, he'd found himself barely able to finish digging the hole.

So, when he'd witnessed a fresh hole being dug recently, and with a victim still in the cellar of his cabin, he'd taken the free labor.

All of them were buried the same, wrapped in a sheet and inside of a wooden trunk. Trunks that the ranger would refer to in his confession, as memory boxes.

<u>Acknowledgements</u>

A massive thanks is owed to my beta readers: Danielle Yeager and Haley Masters. Without their help, this book would have been much more confusing and much less enjoyable.

As for you, I appreciate you more than you know.

Writing is a hell of a time, but it doesn't end up being much fun in the long run, if no one ever reads what you wrote. So thank you to all of you amazing readers and fans. Your support means the world.

Well, onto the next one I suppose.

Whatever that may be.

Echoes of a Fever Dream ©2023

Printed in Great Britain
by Amazon

22320419R00098